Leaving by plane
swimming back underwater

and other stories by
LAWRENCE SCOTT

By the same author

NOVELS

Light Falling on Bamboo

Night Calypso

Aelred's Sin

Witchbroom

SHORT STORIES

Ballad for the New World

NON-FICTION

Golconda, Our Voices Our Lives

Leaving by plane
swimming back underwater

and other stories by
LAWRENCE SCOTT

PAPILLOTE PRESS
London and Trafalgar, Dominica

PRAISE FOR LAWRENCE SCOTT'S SHORT STORIES

The prose is economical and beautifully veined. It is full of light and promise. (Robin Blake, *The Independent on Sunday*)

Lawrence Scott builds his story layer by layer revealing a subtle dependence of character and place and in the process showing an author in control of his form. (Carl MacDougall, *The Scotsman*)

Mighty impressive. (*The Literary Review*)

Scott's language accurately reflects a world, which refuses to slip too easily into any received notions of West-Indianness...Scott reconnects us with the work of Marquez and Jean Rhys. This sensation of retuning linguistic strings alerts us to a new sound in Caribbean prose. (Archie Markham)

Lawrence Scott's stories are a carnival for the senses, conjuring up the images, the sounds, the smells, the tastes, the not-so innocence of childhood and the ambiguities of relationships in a society in the throes of reinventing itself. (Margaret Busby)

Scott's stories are full of lush detail and seedy grandeur...nostalgia is tempered with mockery. (Judy Raymond, *The Sunday Express T&T*)

His descriptive writing is highly detailed, sensual, evocative, yet it serves to carry other elements, examining recent history, politics and the whole make-up of society. (Simon Lee, *The Sunday Guardian T&T*)

For Jenny
My companion in this craft

First published in Great Britain by Papillote Press in 2015

A CIP catalogue record for this book is available from the British Library

Typeset in Minion
Printed in India by Imprint Digital
Design by Andy Dark
Cover design by Andy Dark

ISBN: 978-0-9571187-8-2

Papillote Press
23 Rozel Road
London SW4 0EY
United Kingdom
and Trafalgar, Dominica
www.papillotepress.co.uk
@papillotepress

Contents

Now score
the underlying question on each sheet
and draw a line between the plaited past
and the untangling present.

'Turn The Leaves'
Love for an Island:
the Collected Poems of Phyllis Shand Allfrey

A Little Something

For Harry Jagessar

Walking down our London street under the rowan trees on a quiet Sunday morning, I stopped to interrupt the Indian guy I heard talking to a mate of his while washing his car. 'I hear a little something there,' I said.

'A little something? What's that?' the Indian fella asked.

'A little something, man!'

We had smiled at each other before, but we had never talked. Today we talked, because I had heard that 'little something'. The whole time he was splashing water and wiping fast with his chamois cloth. That's another way I knew something. Like things used to be long time, back home, I thought. He was wringing out the chamois, then he was wiping till the chrome on the hub caps shone.

'Where you from, you must be…from…' I hesitated. I could hear something changing in my own tone now, something I had heard in his.

'From here, man.'

The phrase told me that he wasn't telling me everything. 'From here, yes man, all of we from here now, but I mean where you really from, nuh?' I could hear myself: 'all of we' and 'nuh'.

'Well, my wife…she from Cornwall.'

'I ask about your wife?'

He laughed.

'You know, I hearing a little thing too,' he said, letting

1

himself open up now, smiling, pausing from his rubbing down of the hub caps and looking up at me above the back of his Ford Escort. 'Hmm,' he smiled and chuckled. 'You from Trinidad...' I knew he was convinced, but like he didn't want to be. Something was telling him to doubt. It creased his brow.

'You from Trinidad too,' I said.

We both enjoyed the discovery.

But there was still a look on his face which was him asking himself where this talk was going to go. Like he didn't want to go where it was going.

'Yea. You can hear me then, man.' He acted up the talk a little bit now, enjoying the discovery more. 'The little something...' He winked at his mate now.

'Right,' I said.

'When I first come they ask me if I is Welsh, you know? And I ent even know where Wales is that time,' he laughed.

'Is the song in the talk,' I said.

'Is the lilt in the voice. Calypso, man.' He was truly opening up.

He was finishing the washing of his car. He stopped and laid out the chamois cloth on the bonnet to dry in the hot sun. The summer's day had everyone out in the street. The guy he had been talking to ambled away with, 'I'll see you, Jai,' sensing that we needed to be on our own. And that is how I got to know Jai's name that day.

'So, where you really from then, Jai?' I asked, encouraged to go further.

'You mean back there? Penal?' There was that doubt again, that question, as if I wouldn't know Penal.

'Penal! That is down past Debe.'

'You know Debe?' Jai's surprise was all over his face.

'Yea man, Debe! That is when you come out of San Fernando and you take the road by the savannah in Palmiste, and instead of going straight for Diamond Village, you carry on down to Debe.'

'Boy, Debe…That is where you stop to buy a doubles, where you get polorie and the creole people selling salt fish and accra.'

'Is a Indian cinema, there. You remember flim, boy, how we used to say flim. It right by the junction, almost standing in the cane fields, where the road come down from Picton to Wellington. You know up there? Picton is when you going Barackpore through Monkey Town.'

'You know all them place, boy?' Jai's eyes opened wide.

But that very lack of faith; that doubt that I should know the places which I named, stirred in him, I could see, a certainty, nevertheless, growing in his eyes. It came with the naming; with the saying of the names like mantras which he kept repeating to himself and to me with increasing joy and wonder.

'San Fernando, Picton, Diamond Village, Wellington, Barackpore, Debe, Penal! Boy, is a long time I ent even think of them places, you know.'

As I watched him, I wondered whether it was happening for him as it was for me. The moment he had mentioned Penal it had begun; like a sky opening, or the Atlantic Ocean dividing as the Red Sea had done for Moses, leaving a wide road to the Promised Land.

Watermelons, great green moons were stacked at the back of pick-up trucks alongside the road as you approached the Debe junction. Balancing, wedged between those at the top of the mound were watermelons sliced in half, watery red faces like a sun at sunset. I was truly carried away by the vision places could conjure in a mind sick for home.

'Boy, you living here all this time and we ent even talk. We ent even say how you going, man?' Jai reflected.

'Imagine that!'

'You start me thinking, yes.'

'What you mean? What you thinking 'bout?'

'So where you from then?' he asked.

"Me? I from Sainte Madeleine.'

Jai frowned. 'That's outside San Fernando, going the other way.'

'Yea, Usine, Usine Sainte Madeleine. You pass it when you going Princes Town to Mayaro.'

'Cane. That does take you through the cane. Big sugar factory there.'

'Biggest in the British Empire, they used to say. Yea, that's right, boy, cane. I born and grow up in the cane.'

'How come?' he asked surprised.

'My father managed one of the estates.'

'You father from England?' Jai smiled an ironic smile.

'No man, my parents from there, right back,' I insisted.

'Is so? I looking at you and I say you white but you sounding black. You know what I mean, you sounding like we does sound. You is creole, eh?'

'Yea, my mother is a French creole. Way back. French and Spanish from Caracas with some Carib,' I laughed nervously.

'So is way back, your family?'

'Way, way back. Boy that's home, oui, everybody and everything mix up.'

'Yea, we mix up. Now we mix up. Wasn't always so mix up though. You know what I mean, back then?' Jai watched me closely.

I could see that the sky had also opened up for Jai. The Atlantic Ocean parted its waves and made a big wide road to home in Jai's heart as he stood there in our London street.

'Jai?' I toyed with his name. I was reaching for his whole name. 'Your name…?'

'Harricharan. We from way back too. Way back…Calcutta they tell me.'

'Harricharan! All yuh had a shop in San Fernando?'

'San Fernando? Nah, man, my father's dry goods' store on Penal Main Road.'

'But "Harricharan Brothers", man, you know, on the street going down so to the wharf…Harricharans. Just pass Dutchie's the barbers. They sell them little Dinky cars. I used to collect Dinky cars when I was a boy. You must know Harricharans. There was a Syrian store, maybe Sabga, and Barclay's Bank almost opposite.'

Jai's brow was furrowed like a canefield when they planting new cane. I heard him now again, 'Way back.' I saw him now from the verandah of my home, like one of those Indian boys, cutting and planting cane.

'Boy, you mean Charans.' Jai clicked his fingers. 'They had a book store in the arcade too on Penitence Hill, that steep steep street going up so by the town hall and the court house on Harris Promenade with the statue of Mahatma Gandhi.'

'Is them Hindu names, man. I get mix up. Like Jaggernauth and Jaggesar, Ramchand and Rambachan.'

'We mix you up? We mix you up good, eh? We Indians.' There was something else in Jai's voice; not sweet like sugarcane, but sounding like a bitterness felt by those whose whole life had been a struggle in the cane fields. 'Cane is bitter, the old people used to say,' Jai said.

Here, under the upright rowans of Cressida Road with their berries burnished in the summer sun of England, with the dust blowing up like the dust on a dirt road back there in Penal, Jai and I stood talking on, like there was no time, allowing the deep south of our island to seep into our minds, to explode in our imaginations with the scent of sliced oranges to suck on the side of the street, to conjure a past which we had left a long time ago, back there.

'So, you does go back?' I asked Jai.

'Now and then.'

He looked like I had caught him out, touched a sore spot.

'You up here long?' I asked again.

'A whole life, boy.' I imagined a regret. I heard a little something in his voice which I thought was regret.

'How old when you reach?'

I watched him count the years.

'Fifteen.'

I nearly choked. I saw him first as that small boy at Coffee Street primary school in the churchyard of the Susumachar Presbyterian church in his school uniform; pressed khaki pants and cream cotton short sleeves; Indian boy, Hindu turned Presbyterian. If they had the money, or if he had won a scholarship he would have gone on to Naparima Boys. Fifteen years were enough years to shape the heart, to train the elocution of the voice, so that there would still be that little something we had recognised in each other's speech. I had been the other side of town at the boys' RC school, moved on to Presentation College run by the Irish Brothers.

'Fifteen! Young, boy!'

'My father send us up with our mother; he follow later.' I could hear the ache in the story which was so full of a desire for another kind of future, another kind of life.

'You does go to all them places down south when you go back?'

'Nah! Stay mainly in Port of Spain. Maybe go Chaguanas. Them places rundown now, man,' he said disparagingly. The joy and wonder had gone. The mantras of names had lost their music.

'Yea boy, I know. I was down in the deep south on my last visit. The sea shore eat away, villages run down. And is not only the old fellas drunk on rum leaning up outside the rum shops, you know, but is young guys, out of work, on crack and ganja. And every day is a headline in the newspapers about murder, kidnapping and corruption.'

'Maracas!' Jai shouted out suddenly, as if trying to retrieve what he too sensed we had lost, hitting on a spot you would visit if you stayed up in the north of the island, as if we were tourists, off to the beach. 'Always go there!' His tone was taking in the drive and the views over the mountains to the north coast on the road the Americans had built during the second world war, but knowing we had already lost the joy we had so suddenly found that morning.

I felt that Jai and I could go on like this. But I wondered what we were skirting around, what was it we were not talking about?

'My people from the sugar too, long time, work in the cane. Never was as perfect, you know, as we want to recreate it. That's why my father wanted to get us out. I remember him saying, "The whole place is a blasted sugarcane estate." So, when you say you father managed one of them estates, I smile. I smile how we meeting now.'

It was as if we had sensed right away that we had something to avoid, both born and grown up in the cane, but then realised we no longer had to fear that. Instead of separating us, it had brought us together this summer morning in London; each of us, waiting, alert for any little something in the air which would reconnect us through the sound in a voice to home.

'I going back, you know,' I said, feeling I should hold back because it would start us off again.

'To live?'

I heard the surprise. I knew what he meant. He meant, was I going back to stay permanently. Putting it the way that he had, 'To live?' it sounded as if it was not possible to live there. You could go back and visit. You could stay, off and on. But to live, that would not be possible, living was something we did here, something you did elsewhere: Toronto, Brooklyn.

I had done it myself, left to live a life here, elsewhere. But I also knew that on returning, when the runway came up ahead, my heart would break with the crank of the wheels being let down, and then with the thud as we landed at Piarco. 'Live? Yes man, live!' I dealt with my doubt.

The soft folds of the sugarcane fields among which I had lived and grown up, and which had been fashioned in the image and likeness of another place with names like Arnos Vale and Williamsville, were fast disappearing now; a way of life and culture chopped down, bringing a new meaning to the saying, cane is bitter, as people searched for new work.

Jai listened. 'Live?' He asked himself. 'A little something in that...' He smiled, 'Yea, man!'

A Dog is Buried

I came straight here from the airport in the dark. When we turned off the coastal road, the lights of the taxi lit up the tunnel through the avenue of casaurina trees that led down to the house at the end of the cliff, precipitous, above the sea. And immediately, what had been a distant drumming since Matura, was now a multitudinous, murmuring sea, which, as we stopped in front of the beach house, boomed beneath the cliff, exploding, retreating and then again cannonading. Salt was in the air and the spray was like a fine drizzle.

I had chosen to come back and live near the sea. It had never stopped speaking to me.

We parked along the side of the house.

I asked the taxi driver to wait while I opened up the house. I had not been sure at what time I would eventually get here, so I had not arranged that Walter should be at the house to open it up. I had only arranged that he come up the day before to air the place and put some basics in the fridge. He had forgotten to leave the outside light on, I noticed.

The wind buffeted the coconut trees, twisting their crowns. The cacophony of sea, clattering coconut palms, that whip-lash, the whispering of casaurinas, overwhelmed me as I stumbled into the garage and fumbled for the outside light.

'Gawd, Sir, something stinking up the place,' the taxi driver said behind me.

As he spoke, it was simultaneous with my own exclamation,

'Jesus,' as the awful stench hit me in the face. 'Blast, the fucking bulb has blown. Blast Walter, he could've at least put in a new bulb. What the fuck is that smell?' I stumbled around and fell over a dead weight by the door. I retreated back over a clatter of buckets and gardening implements into the yard where at least there was some light from a quarter moon and I could see the taxi driver bent into the car.

'I has a torch here, Sir, I does keep it for emergency.' He turned from the car and the beam of light picked out a path into the garage, but the source of the stench was still in shadow. 'You take it, Sir. You does swear like crazy, Sir.'

I smiled and took the torch and followed its dim path. 'Jesus, fucking Christ. It stinks.'

'What, Sir?' The taxi driver was at my elbow, looking over my shoulder as I kept the beam on a dead dog, its throat cut, congealing blood oozing out of the wound and soaking into a crocus bag on which it lay. And then I saw the path in the gravel where someone had dragged it into the garage from the yard. I followed the path back with the torch and saw it continued into the gravel of the yard where the crocus bag had been dragged, and the path disappeared as the light exhausted its strength. Who on earth had pulled it all this way, and why?

I heard the car starting up and saw the taxi driver turning it around. 'Hang on, my bags are still in the car.' I ran after him. He stopped, turned, and then started coming towards me. I jumped out of the way.

'Is OK, Sir.' He leant out of the window. 'I just turn it to let the car light shine into the garage.'

Someone had dragged the dog all this way. But when? Surely Walter was supposed to have been here yesterday. I fought for the keys in my shoulder bag to see whether the house had been made clean for my welcome home.

'Let me take a bulb from in the house, Sir, and put in this empty socket for you.'

'Of course, it's empty, Walter hasn't been here. This animal has been dead for at least a day.' It was in fact decomposing in the heat. It had black fur with white patches around the neck and legs. Once, someone's pet, or one of the stray mongrels which you often saw on the beaches up the coast. It looked fat, not scrawny, like the beach dogs which pestered people scavenging for scraps of food. You could play cuatro on their rib bones. It was bloated with decomposition.

Then I could see maggots like creamy pearls issuing from its putrefying mouth and the wound in its neck. 'Who would cut a dog's throat?' I stepped over the corpse into the kitchen and turned on the light. The illumination lit up the dead thing in all its wondrous, enigmatic horror. As I stepped over it, I almost felt irreverent now, like crossing over the corpse of a person. I went into the house turning on lights and opening doors with my bunch of keys. Nothing appeared to be disturbed, but the house smelt musty, with mildew, dust and cobwebs and the furniture was sticky with the residue of sea blast. No air had penetrated here for months, only that which battered its way through the jalousie cracks and hinges from the howling sea breeze on the verandah side. I opened the big door onto the verandah. It was like letting in a hurricane. The sea, like a great dark beast came in, rolling and crawling over the rocks. Then it multiplied into a multitude of serpents. I lost them under the cliff, but heard their hissing, then again, the pounding and the drumming insistence.

I was home. But what did this dead dog mean? What did it signify, if anything? Why would someone put it there, apparently so deliberately? The taxi driver was staring down at the dead dog, now seemingly impervious to the stench that to some extent was dissipated by the gusts of sea breeze blowing through the house.

'Look, I've not paid you. How much do I have for you? You must want to go.'

'Is, is fifty dollars, Sir. But I go help you. Let me take this dog outside for you. I go put it in the trunk and dump it for you.'

I fumbled for my wallet and gave him the notes with a ten-dollar tip. 'No, come on, if you're going to take it away, here's another twenty. You sure. God, that would be great.'

There was a sudden relief. We each took a corner of the crocus bag and dragged the corpse towards the back of the car, stumbling backwards, the torch moving about like erratic spotlight in a cheap pantomime. 'Let me get the keys to open the trunk,' the taxi driver said.

The weight was horribly dead and my fingers touched its grizzly stiff leg. I was repulsed, I stood back from where it lay.

'Hang on, let me get my bags out.' I took one, the taxi driver the other. We put them down at the entrance of the garage. Then we heaved the dead weight and lay it in the trunk, rigor mortis had set in long ago, the stiff leg jammed against the inside of the trunk as we forced it down and slammed the door shut.

There was a trail of black blood across the garage floor. I swashed it down with Dettol and masses of washing-up liquid frothing in a bucket.

'I don't even know your name. Out of nowhere, you drive me here. God I've just arrived from England, what the hell's the time, what a welcome. What a homecoming. I'm Christian.' I extended my arm to shake his hand. We shook hands. 'Christian de la Borde. Chris, a cousin calls me Chris, I prefer the whole of my name. You might know the name, my grandfather had estates near here, de la Borde…'

'Leopold, Sir, Callender, Leopold Callender, I from Sangre Grande. My grandfather work on an estate up there. Maybe our grandfathers knew each other.'

I smiled. I suddenly hoped our grandfathers had known each other. A thought. I felt close to Leopold Callender. A wild thought. 'Sangre Grande? A lot of blood?'

'Yes, Sir, it bleed a lot.'

'Yes, no, I mean, not the dog, Sangre Grande, Spanish, the name, a lot of blood. There was once a massacre there, a long time ago, I mean a long, long time ago and a lot of blood was spilt. History. Come, take a drink nuh? Rum or whisky, I've got some whisky somewhere, duty free, before you go down, before you take that dog and dump it. You sure you go manage that on your own?'

'Yes, man. History? You does study history? I see you have a lot of books. It important.'

'Yes, my bags are bulging, and more to come, an entire library.' I got out some glasses and put the rum and whisky on the dresser.

We both chose rum. 'I go pass back for the whisky,' Leopold Callender laughed. 'The rum will do me for now.'

Leopold Callender stood out on the verandah where the wind was tearing at the folded canvas awning and rattling the hinges. He had his back to me. I noticed now that he was a tall man, broad shoulders, but slim at the waist. Strong legs. Hard, tight, curved buttocks. His thick African hair was plaited and curled into locks which reached his neck line, a thick mass, they moved as one when he turned his head, and now as the wind caught them. He must be about thirty, I thought.

The dead dog had thrown us together. He had been helpful, and intending to take the dog away. Snippets of reports drifted up into my mind, from letters to London from friends about how the coast had changed, was changing. It was no longer safe. There were burglaries, rapes and drug smuggling. There had been a shooting. These thoughts raced through my mind now.

But Leopold was being so helpful. He was charming. I hadn't really had a good look at him before. All of our talk was mostly in the dark. I could hardly see him in the muted lights of the airport car park, the taxi drive up, during which I nodded off between snatches of polite talk and then noticing the reminders of where we were, looming up in the beam of the car lights; the bridge at Salibia, the sea, looking down to the mouth of the river. I liked the way he talked, and he seemed exceedingly polite, helpful. These thoughts kept racing through my mind as I poured more rum out. 'Here, one for the ancestors, the spirits. Here, a libation.'

Leopold turned towards me where he was standing and I let a few drops of rum pour out of the bottle on to the floor. 'Not like the earth, won't soak it up. Ice?'

I noticed my open wallet on the dresser, bulging with pound notes.

'You is a real Trinidadian? You know about them old-time things. I go take it straight.'

I plonked a couple of ice cubes into my own glass, wondering how old the water was. Had Walter been here? There was no food, but the fridge was clean and turned on. I ignored the mystery of Walter. 'Here you are.' I handed Leopold his glass of rum, joining him on the verandah, looking out to the dark sea, tinged with the faint moonlight. 'Cheers.' We clinked glasses. We smiled. He was a handsome man. Very black skin. High cheekbones, shining. Very white teeth. I liked his face. He was younger than me, but I felt that he was older. Maybe, because I needed him, was depending on him to get rid of the dead dog.

We both sighed as the rum warmed our chests.

'You can't beat the Old Oak,' Leopold laughed.

I felt that now, suddenly, since we had taken care of the dead dog, he was trying to make conversation, to go further than the business we had had to deal with.

'In the boom time, you know rum sales went down, more people was drinking whisky than rum.'

'Incredible, I know, those years. Different now. Those must be the oil flares down Galeota way.' The horizon was a haze of orange light.

'Yea, somebody making money.'

'I'm really grateful, about the dog.'

'Nothing, man. Glad to help out.'

'But, must be something wrong, I can't imagine why somebody would kill a dog, slit its throat and then drag it up that hill, and dump it in front of an empty beach house, my beach house.'

'You never know what does go on. All kind of different thing going on now.'

'It's like some kind of threat, don't you think? Some kind of warning, of what's going to happen. But, from whom? I've not been living here for a year, and before that I've only come on visits. I can't imagine what it has to do with me. It's like a bad Hollywood movie.'

'I don't think is you, Sir...'

'Christian. Call me Christian.'

'Chris, Christian. I think it must be...Who is Walter? I hear you mention, Walter.'

'He looks after the house for me when I'm away. He's from down the road in Rampanalgas, you know. Walter is a Rampanalgas boy. I've known him since he was young. I know his father and mother. I know the family. They worked on the estate.'

'So, where he is? He ent been up here man, has he? You say he was supposed to bring food, turn on lights. Where he is? I feel this dog is to do with Walter.'

I drew out two of the old verandah deck chairs and opened them out for Leopold and myself. Leopold sat down. I went and got the bottle of rum and poured him another shot and then one for myself. We speculated about Walter. I began to wonder why Leopold didn't leave. I was beginning to feel really tired. I must have fallen off to sleep. I woke suddenly. The sea was booming beneath the cliff.

'Africa...'

'What? What? Where am I?'

'Is OK, Christian. You right here.' Leopold reached out to steady me, putting his hand on my shoulder, as I nearly fell out of the deck chair. 'You fall asleep for a couple of seconds. Is OK.'

'Right.'

'I was just saying that between here and Africa there is no land.'

I looked out at the dark and empty sea. Then I saw the oil flares.

I found my bearings.

'The coast goes along that way. But straight ahead is Africa.' Then Leopold changed his tone. 'I change my mind.'

'What?'

'I going to bury that dead dog now.'

'What? Now?'

'Yea, I see you have fork and spade in the garage. Won't take long.'

I was confused, exhausted, now frightened. The night, the early morning, whatever it was, was speeding away in front of me with the jet lag. My adrenalin was high.

Stars, like stars are in tropical skies, hung like huge planets. Then the gauze of the Milky Way glittered on endlessly, part of another coast.

I had imagined the whole thing before it had taken place. Classical déjà vu.

Two men, one black, one white, go into the dark, into the bushes under the coconut trees where the earth is soft, not too far from the edge of the cliff, but far enough that the grave won't collapse into the sea within a month, delivering its skeleton onto the pebbled beach below to join with the driftwood, plastic bottles, old tyres, on the beach. One digs, the other shovels, then they switch over, sharing the different labours. A bottle of rum and two glasses are on the ledge of rock nearby. They rest, have a shot of rum and then continue with their grave. They pause, look out to the sea. They sip rum. The coconut palms clatter out their lamentations and psalms. The breakers drum below the cliff. A ripe coconut hits the ground, budup. The grave grows deeper. They are both pouring with sweat. They take their shirts off. Their sweat is a dew on their brows and arms, a libation into the hole in the ground. They finish. There is a mound of earth on the side of the grave. They stick the shovel and spade into it. They sit and look out to the sea. The breeze comes in and cools them. They shiver. They lean against each other; their naked backs against each other, their faces, one towards the hills, the other to the sea. Together, they look both ways, as if at a cross roads. They don't know each other. But on this night they are not just themselves, and they know they've met before, when ancestors acted differently.

They bury a dead dog.

Leopold and Christian go to the car. Leopold opens up the trunk and they lift out the stinking dead dog and cradle it as if in a hammock. They walk stumblingly back to the grave. They dump the dog and crocus bag into the grave. Christian hurries back to the house and fills a bucket with water and Dettol and throws it over the animal. The stench is unbearable. They turn to the sea and inhale deep breaths of salty air. Then they shovel madly, then beat down the earth. One of the dog's legs keeps sticking out of the earth. Eventually, after repeated lashes with the fork and shovel, they break the leg and complete the filling in of the grave.

The two men had different reasons for burying the dog.

I am a young boy, fourteen. My dog, Kim, has died. A man is helping me dig a grave under the mango tree in the bungalow yard up on the hill. All around there is the silence of the day-time forest. We can't get the dog to fit into the grave. The more we throw earth on the grave the more the dog springs up.

I turn away. I cry. The man puts his hand on my shoulder. He is my father. Another man is there, a friend of my father's. There is a man from the estate. We try again, but we can't bury the dead dog.

There was another part to my memory…

I woke. Where was I? Then…

The sunlight was crashing through the open window facing the sea. The breeze was cool, but warming. I had no idea what the time was. Must be mid-morning, I thought. There was an intense silence, except for the sea, the clatter of the coconut palms and casaurinas whispering, that peculiar orchestra of the cliff-side with my old beach house, part of the old estate. It was so primal this space: sunlight, the sea, coconuts, casaurinas and the tall tall palmistes. I lay naked, the sheets all in a heap on the floor.

Leopold? The dead dog? What had happened? I leapt up, pulling on my pants, and dashed into the corridor and out to the living room. My wallet was still on the kitchen dresser bulging with pound notes. Then I saw there were two letters still on the floor kicked behind the door. One was from Pip, the other from Marianne. I then remembered their last visit when they had lain naked on their beds asleep and a man had entered their room and held a knife to Marianne's throat. I could not get them to join me again from England. I anchored the letters under a vase on the dining-room table. The rooms were full of light and breeze. The whole house was opened up and part of the outside, shimmering with light and green and blue and ochre. It was a tight, hot, dry-season day. The whole island opened up in my chest. I was glad to be home. No Leopold. The car was still there. The front door was open. The trunk was open.

'Leopold!' I shouted. He was nowhere in the immediate yard. Then I saw the whole place for the first time in the light. The spaces under the almond trees. The cliff-side falling to the sea that I had to do something about. Sea-grapes and almond trees twisted and rusty with the salt from the blast. The huge, huge blue sky. Tight and blue. 'Leopold!'

I was walking on the gravel like a child does, barefoot. I

walked towards where we had dug the grave and buried the dead dog. Ti-Marie with her sharp pikànt closed her leaves to my footfall. I picked my way to the clearing. The night returned, our digging and burying. 'Leopold!' I presumed he must be here. I went to the front, to the steps off the verandah, which descended to the beach and the rock pool where you could swim when the tide was in. From the top of the steps I looked down the coast to Matura's high sand dunes where the birthing turtles came up at night, further along to Manzanilla and then the curve disappeared. I could see the sugar loaf of Tamana. I started walking down the concrete steps. Must fix these, I thought. They were eroded. The blast reached here in rough seas. Salt in the air, on my tongue. So much to do, now that I was back for good. For good? It sounded kind of final and frightening, thrilling and frightening. 'Leopold.' He was at the edge of the water. He was standing then stooping, like a tall heron, I thought. He bent and touched the water with his fingers the way I did as a child, the water in the holy-water font and signed myself with the cross. Some things in life don't change. He dived, and dived again, and then having heard my cry, he stood in the half deep and looked up at me on the steps and waved, shaking the water from his Rasta locks.

'Chris!' He shouted.

I took the steps, two at a time, and was on the small jetty of rock and cement. Mossy steps descended into the water. Every part of this space reverberated with my childhood. I learnt to walk along this jetty, each small step recalled on these paving stones. I learnt to swim here, to take my first dive. And all the years I had been coming back here after going to England were jumbled up in my mind. I walked down into the sea and dived. 'Hi', coming up spluttering.

'Chris, man, this is really beautiful here.'

'You stayed the night?'

'Battery run down. We leave the light on, man. In all the excitement. That dam dog.'

'You know, I noticed the lights on, I meant to say something. Well, where did you sleep?'

'I just lay down right there on the sofa in the drawing room. You sleep like a log. I come in to see if you awake, you just sleeping like an innocent baby.' He smiled. 'You'll get a tan soon in this hot sun.' He looked at my white body.

I don't know why I did it, but I jetted some water at him, spraying over his face and shoulders, water-fight like when I was a boy. I laughed out loud. I felt so happy. I was so glad that he had not left, that he had spent the night. 'Just lay down on the sofa.'

'I'm glad you stayed.' I sprayed him again with the surf.

He laughed and jetted white water at me. We dived and swam out past the entrance to the rock pool where the sea swelled up and broke on itself. We turned and belly-surfed back in, paddling wildly with our hands and feet. Our bodies tumbled onto a shoal.

'There may be only black coffee for breakfast.' I climbed up the mossy steps and said, looking over my shoulder, 'See you at the house.'

Leopold brought in some coconuts and we had coconut water first. Then we had the black coffee. Afterwards we kick-started the car and Leopold drove me to Cumana to get some basics at the Chiney shop. I was putting off my inquiry into Walter's whereabouts, and what to do about the dog. Should I go and see the police? Leopold advised against that, but said we could go down to Rampanalgas afterwards. I decided I would walk to Rampanalgas in the afternoon. I advised Leopold to make the journey to Sangre Grande without stopping though the battery did seem recharged after the drive to Cumana.

'You must pass in,' I said as we shook hands.

'Yes, man, you go see me again, Christian.'

'Leopold.' I touched his arm affectionately.

He smiled, waved, and then I lost sight of him and the car as it entered the casaurina avenue.

We buried it. Yes, we buried it. A dog is buried.

I felt exhausted. Still jet-lagged. Fear crept up on me, now that I was alone. I was disturbed by the welcome I had had. I would have to go into Rampanalgas; I was putting it off. When it was cooler I would walk down. I strung up the hammock on the verandah and slept all afternoon. Dusk. The sky along the coast bled all the way to the horizon.

I felt like eating some fish. I noticed that some fishermen still used the rocks in the other bay. I went down and called to one of them to sell me one of their catch. He smiled. He had sold to us before. I did not know his name.

'So, Miss Marianne gone back.' He cleaned the red snapper on the rocks with his knife, slitting the gullets, gutting the fish and swishing it in the surf on the rocks.

Blood, and white lace. *Hic est sanguis meus.*

'Oh, yes.' It was she who had started getting fish here. 'Yes, she's gone back.'

Blood on a white linen sheet…Why that thought?

That was the other part of my dream. Marianne standing on the rocks looking out to sea. The sun on her shoulders. Freckled shoulders. That was it…

The white linen sheet stained with blood…

'Them fellers who does fish asking for she.' The fisherman looked up from his filleting. 'She promise them…'

'What? What did she promise them?' I shouted above the breakers on the black rocks. The answer was the repeated boom of the sea with its long memory of raping, killing and burying, the blood from the gutted fish staining the rocks.

Tales Told under
the San Fernando Hill

1
The Architect and his Wife

'He's in the orchid house, Madam,' the old nurse, Justine, called from the courtyard where she sat overlooking the gulf, sewing and tending the memories of her madam's daughters.

'Leave him, Justine, with his toothbrush. Soon he'll even forget that, and I'll have to keep them alive.' Emilia Calderon continued to mend her husband's old khaki pants, seeing him as Justine had described, cleaning the leaves of his precious orchids with his old toothbrush, in case blight crinkled their leaves and stunted their growth.

When Carlos Calderon, the architect of San Fernando, was not in his office at his drawing board, level with the sill of the Demerara window overlooking the wharf with the sloops waiting to be loaded with sugar, he would spend what seemed like an eternity in his orchid house. It seemed like this to his wife, Emilia, whom he had married when she was sixteen. So, now that her daughters themselves had married and left home, she was still a young woman with a whole life to live, while he seemed more and more like an old man.

Emilia never let that thought enter too deeply into her imagination, otherwise she would have to go and confess to the parish priest, Father Muller, the terrifying fantasies which were unleashed in her mind; things she had not thought it possible that she could imagine, that anyone could imagine. Where did these imaginings bloom? How, out of nothing? How, with the kind of mother and father she had had, could she imagine such…? She hated to think of them, and then of course it made her think of them even more. For days, they became inescapable; obsessions, like some dark flower, some deadly nightshade growing as black as purple in her brain.

'Bless me Father, for I have sinned.'
  'My daughter?'
  'Father, it's a month since my last confession.'
  'My daughter?'
  'Father, they've come again. Last night it was the boy first of all, in the garden under the bougainvillea arbour, as brown and as smooth as a young deer, his mouth wet; so wet and smooth, I could feel his hot breath smelling of guavas on my neck where he stood naked as the day he was born; standing there, looking up at my window with the moonlight on his face; his face like an angel's; his limbs and torso as natural to the garden as the limbs of the orange trees and the bark of the cedars.'
  The priest wondered at the woman's flight of words.
  'I felt the walls of the house dissolve and the garden rise up, carrying him into my room, into my bed. First it was the boy. But then, the girl, Father. I had not known that desire until she was in my arms like one of my daughters at first, and then Father that other desire. Then they were together again and stayed in the garden together and played till I could watch it no longer, the unspeakable things they did with each other, that I had to leave the window and kneel at the prie-dieu and ask the Blessed Therese, the Little Flower, to intercede on my behalf. It used to work when I was small, Father. I think it did. It does not seem to now. Nothing seems to work now. And I'm

a grown up woman now, Father. Why did it work then, the way of perfection?'

'My child?'

'My husband, Father. He remembers nothing. What must I do about the boy, Father? And, what about the girl?

'My daughter, there are other penitents in the line, you must stop and say ten Hail Marys for the salvation of those souls still in purgatory. Keep praying to the Little Flower.'

'Yes, Father.'

Meanwhile, Carlos Calderon had continued all that afternoon in the shade of the orchid house where the angelhair fern grew in the moist soil between the pebbles of the pathways. He continued to scrub the fleshy leaves of the epiphytes with his old toothbrush. All of his life now was consumed in this horticulture.

Justine was still at her look-out in the courtyard. Her sewing had fallen from her lap and she had nodded off into the daydreams of a woman who had come as far as this on her own, tending her madam's affairs and her madam's daughters as if they had been her own. Somewhere in her humming, with which she had comforted those little girls in their growing up, was a lamentation, which came into her voice and sounded like the surf of the sea, swelling and breaking on the shore with the cries of her ancestors.

2

The Women of the Legion of Mary

'Who it is? So long they have Father in there listening, when so many people want to confess.'

'Is Mistress Calderon, Mistress Redhead. You didn't see

Father call her out of her pew when he come inside the church?' Mrs Nunez said. 'She don't have to line up.'

'I bet I know what she have to confess. People that have she colour skin have only one thing to confess, pride and greed.'

'That is two things,' Mrs Nunez chipped in. 'And is colour of skin that determining sin now? You know life tell me that all kind of people capable of all kind of things. What you calling sin? I believe that some of them is not even sin.'

'That is what I have to say, you can believe what you like.' Mistress Redhead took a kerchief out off her bosom, emitting the odour of talcum powder and bay rum, to wipe her black brow and fan herself in the heat.

'You think is only pride and greed they have to confess? They must have ordinary sins like other people.' Mrs Nunez, a coco 'panol, winced a little at what she saw might be an implied attack on her own mixed blood by the black woman. She had also heard her berating the Venezuelan girls who came from down the main. 'Them red-skin girls think they pretty, them who dance those lewd dances in the clubs on the wharf of San Fernando.' Mrs Nunez did not want to be confused with those girls, though she was proud of her Venezuelan ancestry, her father coming to the island to work the cocoa in the Montserrat hills. She knew what people said, that some of them were not real girls, only play-play girls, them boys that does like to dress up like girls.

'Ordinary sins? Sin is not ordinary, child, sin is…,' and Mistress Redhead broke off and turned her eyes to the life-size crucifix above the high altar, leaving Mrs Nunez to imagine what sin could be if it was not ordinary.

Mistress Redhead, as she examined her conscience before entering the confessional box, thought that sin was like life, that part of your life, which did not go so good. How could sin be the same for her as for Mistress Calderon? While Mistress Calderon lived on the morne, the highest peak before the summit of San Fernando Hill, in a house reaching beyond itself with turrets and balconies, grand staircases and bay windows, decorated with fretwork and the lace of lattice; its terraces falling away to lawns and sunken gardens under orange trees, Mistress Redhead lived behind the Radio City cinema in Rushworth Street, not far from Paradise cemetery, in a small gingerbread house, a miniature conception of grandeur, at least on the outside. While it was not the lowest part of town, it was still too near to the market in Mucurapo Street where life was such a confusion day and night that it would be impossible for her to imagine what sin meant there.

Mistress Redhead had long ago got rid of her husband. She kept Eldridge's name, Redhead, because of her children, but, now, she unassailably raised her head as she walked down the street and made sure she was known as Mistress Redhead. Though she knew that people knew why she threw Eldridge out of the house - for philandering and adultery with those same Venezuelan girls who hung out of the balcony above Chen's shop on the corner of Mucurapo and Coffee Street, giggling behind those silly fans Chen had imported from Hong Kong. She herself had heard the rumour that those girls got up to all kind of things with themselves. But Mistress Redhead did not want to think about that. It was bad enough to think of Elridge with one of them, or two of them or whatever numbers it was.

She felt it deeply, and the memory of Elridge Redhead's skin was like velvet to her touch.

And, as if Mrs Nunez knew what was in Mistress Redhead's thoughts, she expressed what was going on in her own head, thinking aloud. 'You know they say some of them girls is not really girls at all. Them is play-play girls, them soft-face boys from down the main in pretty shirts and tight pants who like to wine they bamsie in the street, as they swing that purse they have in their hand.' The line of a calypso ran through her head, 'Norman is that you...' Mrs Nunez lowered her voice, holding back from literally bursting out into full voice for the rendition of the calypso. She had gone beyond her thoughts with talking them aloud.

'What you talking about girl?' The terrible thought was that Eldridge had not only gone with one or two or three of them girls from the balcony of Chen's shop, but that one of them might not have been a girl at all. 'Eldridge!'

She chose to return to her previous thread of thought, her honour and dignity. This was not the sin of pride, she thought, this was dignity to deport herself in this way now.

Was her sin envy, as she tried to raise her self-esteem and her income with the piano lessons she gave bright boys and girls from the convent and the Catholic college? Was it envy that made her house shine with polish and new linoleum, bright waxened flowers in the green cut-glass vase on the centre table, placed expertly on the crocheted doily mat? Or, was it dignity?

Mistress Redhead examined her conscience. She grew philosophical. She was a teacher in the school built against the walls of the church of Notre Dame de Bon Secours where Indian children, smart in mathematics, smelling of coconut oil, laboured their way out of the sugarcane fields where their parents cut cane. Sin and history, thought Mistress Redhead. Did one absolve the other?

She had kept her eyes fixed on the crucifix where the nails fastened the hands and feet of her saviour to the wood of the cross.

Could she hold Mistress Calderon responsible for that crime? On Good Friday, in the service of the mass of the Pre-Sanctified, they used to say the Jews were responsible. Then she had read what terrible things the Nazis had done to the Jews. Then you see, the logic led her to herself and her own people and Mistress Calderon's part in the whole thing; the calamitous holocaust of the Middle Passage, that long procession of charnel galleons. History and poetry lifted Mistress Redhead's pride. She found beautiful lines in difficult books for difficult subjects in Mr Sealey's bookshop in the arcade on Penitence Hill. Mistress Redhead's grandfather had the story almost first hand, and she wondered if he, in his time, had gone up to the great house on the morne and killed those whom he found in there at the time, whether that would've been a sin to crucify her saviour, or an act to liberate her people? Mistress Redhead scared herself with her speculations.

The fleeting thought from her conversation with Mrs Nunez flickered to bring her down from the heights of her philosophical speculation. Eldridge with one of them buller boys? She had never ever spoken the word and she looked about her as if her thought might have been heard. My God! Things had become worse in this world.

'Morne,' she gathered herself, reflecting aloud, sounding her sadness with a moan. 'While it means a little hill, also means sadness in classical French,' Mistress Redhead said melancholically to Mrs Nunez as she moved off to kneel in the confessional to confess her sins to Father Muller.

'What you say Mistress Redhead? Where you does get these things from? I ent catch what you say, nuh.' Mrs Nunez fixed her mantilla on her head and resumed her posture for prayer, but was too distracted by Mistress Redhead and her ideas of other people and things. She kept seeing those pretty boys from down the main wining their bamsie in the High Street as if is carnival. And is not only the boys from down the main, is all of them, young black fellas, Indians, French creole, Syrian, Chiney, the lot. She might be happier if she minded her own business, Mrs Nunez thought quietly to herself.

3
The First Kiss

When the Calderon house on the morne was silent, and Emilia and Carlos were asleep at siesta time, and Justine was resting on her iron bed in the servants' room off the courtyard, and this world seemed like on another planet to Rushworth Street and Mucurapo Street in down-town San Fernando, children stole into the garden to play. These were children who lived on the morne in the neighbouring houses beneath San Fernando Hill, among the orchards of guava trees, which bore enormous fragrant fruit full of pink seeds on which maggots liked to feed. The boys scraped out the seeds and the maggots and filled the pink cup of pulp with brown sugar, to gorge themselves on the confection.

In the silence of the early afternoon, before Carlos went back to his drawing board in his office overlooking the wharf and the sloops loaded with sacks of sugar, and Emilia went to her Legion of Mary Praesidium meeting at five o'clock, Guillaume and Pierre, two of the children, played in the hot and silent garden. They crept up from their houses under the guava trees and played in the orchid house, in the mango orchard, among the anthuriums and under the bougainvillea arbours at the bottom of the terraces where the giant cacti unfurled their dangerous tendrils. They played in the grotto of the Madonna Dolorosa and the shaded courtyard of this mysterious garden - a forbidden place.

Le Petit Morne was a magnet. Beneath the hill the traffic in the town of San Fernando droned like a swarm of bees punctuated by the blare of car horns and the high voices of Chutney music over the tassa drums.

In the presbytery, next to the church, Father Muller snored the sleep of a priest exhausted by the sins of the town, and his own peccadillos.

The boys should have been in their rooms, resting as their mothers thought, if not actually sleeping. They should have been reading comic books quietly: Batman, Captain Marvel, Wonderwoman and Superman - a pantheon of Americana.

This prowling around the garden in the heat of the afternoon was illicit. They fought and played and grew together, their bodies changing, their sex flourishing without any idea of the sins that plagued Mistress Redhead or Emilia Calderon, or for that matter, Father Muller.

In the hot and still afternoon, they did not think of the fires of hell or of mortal sin. Those thoughts and fears would come in the night, if they came at all, and they would have to go to sleep in their parents' bed and be given hot cocoa to drink with vanilla mixed in to soothe and quieten their fear. They would have to be given the rosary, and be told to say an act of contrition and make a firm purpose of amendment; sent off to sleep folded in the wings of their guardian angels until Father Muller could absolve them in the morning before the six o'clock mass, for they had arrived at the age of reason, made their First Communions and were just about to be confirmed.

But really they had just been children as any enlightened person would know; boys together, fascinated by the little pleasure growing between their legs and the pleasure they gave themselves and each other if they touched those little totees, if they stroked them with soft and gentle fingers, licked them with sticky tongues. All boys have known these peccadillos with each other and joked boastfully of them when they are drunken men. 'Man, and you rub totee together when you was a boy!'

These were not sins. These were not nails to be driven into the hands of Mistress Redhead's saviour on the cross.

Cockerels crowed in the afternoon, defying the prescribed dawn, three times even, suggesting a denial and betrayal the boys did not understand.

Then in the loft above the servants' quarters where Justine was sleeping; in this loft where chickens liked to roost so that the floor was soft with moulted feathers, nests of warm eggs, the boys lay in the stillness of the hot afternoon, drawn here by their play and innocence.

Guillaume and Pierre lay on their backs and looked up at the low ceiling in which they saw little dots of light in the darkness; like the stars at night in an immense sky. Constellations, galaxies! Their eyes smarted from flecks of dust falling, held in the gossamer cobwebs.

Justine snored and dreamt her old woman's dreams in the room below. She dreamt of cane fields and a mother's ambition that her daughter would not break her back with that labour.

'Let me lie on top of you,' Guillaume whispered.

They had never done that before and Pierre felt that he could not breathe.

'Let me kiss you,' Guillaume whispered again, 'as if you were a girl.'

'But I'm a boy,' Pierre protested, and then let himself slip into an idea of himself as a girl as Guillaume positioned himself.

'Let me kiss you anyway. Pretend.' And he put his lips on Pierre's and then having never learnt this, they began to feel the tips off their tongues in each other's mouths and soon they were going deeper with their sighs.

'This is like in the films,' Pierre said breathlessly, enjoying the pretence. 'Like Lana Turner with Rock Hudson.'

'Like Burt Lancaster and Deborah Kerr in *From Here to Eternity*.'

'On the beach in see-through swimming costumes which Father Muller says is immoral.'

'Does he?'

'He told me that in confession.'

Without much thought, the boys had undressed each other in what now was truly a kind of passion, Pierre's clothes now discarded. Their brown bodies were stuck with white chickens' feathers in the dim light of stars, glowing with the aura of the Hollywood screen.

4

The Architect's Words

'Those children, again,' said Emilia to Carlos as their breakfast was ending and he was peeling a ripe banana to put out on the tray for the birds. He was not listening to her and she felt that he had now enough excuses, which he could use for his lack of attention, and not feel that he had neglected her, but just that he could not help it. Doctor Maillot had told Emilia on the phone that Carlos was seriously ill.

'You said something?' Carlos cut open grapefruits and ripe mangos for the birds' platter, and already the blue tanagers, the yellow-breasted keskidee, the palm tanagers and the blue streaks of the blue jeans were darting in for their morning feed.

'Those children who come to play here. I'm worried. Yesterday after siesta, I saw them crawling out of the loft above Justine's room covered with feathers. They were naked and were washing the feathers off their bodies at the standpipe by the orchid house. What do you make of that?'

'Unsure of who they are they're pretending to be birds, but it didn't work out. You sure it's not one of your dreams?'

'Dreams? What dreams? Why don't they know who they are?'

'Do we really know who we are?'

Immediately he said this, she saw his back disappearing into his study where she knew he would be cloistered for an hour with his stamps before he went into the orchid house. Horticulture came after philately, and then came architecture at his drawing board overlooking the wharf.

Dreams: what did he know of her dreams? They weren't dreams, they were thoughts, or, yes, daydreams, when she was on her own overlooking the garden as she had been doing at the end of siesta, and seen Pierre and Guillaume emerging from the loft encrusted with birds' feathers. Or, they were visions. Father Muller said they were bad thoughts. She did see the boys, she couldn't help seeing them if they were in her garden when she looked out of her bedroom window. What had they to do with the boy and girl whom she saw doing their unspeakable acts; his breath hot on her neck, his body wet like a young deer? And she? Who was she, the girl who came into her bed and lay in her arms bringing that desire?

Only confession gave respite to the laryngitis, which Emilia continued to suffer because of her inability to speak out about the world of her dreams and feelings.

Justine found it hard to hear and so to understand what was going on for her madam, but she guessed from the look on her face that it was the distress she had seen there ever since her last daughter, Giaconda, had got married and left the house, leaving her alone with her husband. Justine watched the confusion on her young madam's face. It was not something she had ever allowed herself to experience. She preferred to keep herself to herself. She would be content with the married girls coming back to visit and in time bringing their own children to her. That would be sufficient, she told herself. Hers was the nurse's story.

5
The Women of the Legion of Mary

'You hear the news? Mistress Calderon's husband dead,' Mrs Nunez announced.

'Is so?' Mistress Redhead said. 'I didn't know he was sick. To tell you the truth I never really see him. I sure he must be there in the front pew with she Sunday mass, but I never really see him, is always she I see, and then she used to have daughters but they gone and get married. So long she not come to meetings. So, she on she own now. Well, that is something in the big house, all on she own. But she is a young woman. She could married again.'

'They say all he arteries clog up with the smoking. The blood couldn't get to Mr Calderon's brain. Is that he dead of?'

'An ordinary death.'

'What you mean, an ordinary death?'

'Well, he ent dead of anything really special, like say, a lingering and gradually debilitating disease which eventually send him mad so that he roam the streets and bring shame on the family and town.'

'You have an imagination, yes, Mistress Redhead, and you could speak some words sometimes. Trouble with all you teachers. I think he dead of quite a grand death, fading away. Some people does dead just so, you know. Nothing, they just die. But your arteries clog up so the blood can't flow?'

'Is so I want to die. Drop my neck so like a fowl, and when they feel my pulse, I done gone already.' She laughed.

'You feeling lucky? You know what some people does say about death, that your whole life at the moment of your death, that it all come back from the time you is a tiny child to whenever it catch you, old, young, middle age, anyhow.'

'You believe that? But you will have an extraordinary death, Mistress Redhead. I feel so for sure.'

'It sound like it could happen. But Father Muller say you have to live every moment as if you going to die at any time. He comes like a thief in the night, is what the gospel say. You mustn't go back in your house to fetch your coat. When death call, you just have to go.'

'Is so I want it. I 'fraid suffering, and I ent have no coat. And they say in the end, Mr Calderon had to suffer, and she, his young wife, because she younger than he, had to sit by the bed for days with her daughters, while he suffered. He had tubes to help him breathe from the oxygen tank. He was in a coma. They say people does hear when they in a coma. You have to be careful what you say, because they could suddenly wake up like Lazarus, I suppose, and if you not saying something you want them to hear, it could be really embarrassing.' Mrs Nunez went on with her anxiety. She would not like people to be hearing the thoughts she did not care to express, like telling Mistress Redhead about the play-play girls in their pretty shirts and tight pants.

The women talked of suffering, dying and death. Sins were again confessed, nails driven into the saviour were released with forgiveness and Father Muller's absolution.

6
Rita Hayworth's Kiss

The next time that Emilia Calderon spotted the two children again emerging from the loft above Justine's room, she wanted to call out. She had learnt their names from Justine. She felt transfixed. She could not run to her husband in shock to say that they had transformed themselves into birds. She remained at the windowsill of her bedroom looking down into the courtyard, as one of them, whom she thought must be Pierre, because the other one still looked like the boy Guillaume, whom Justine had pointed out, was finding it difficult to get out of the window of the loft. What in fact she saw emerging from the window gradually was what looked to her like a giant chrysalis. The two small feet in silver shoes encrusted with sequins dangled from beneath a profusion of chiffon and tulle and hooped crinolines. Emerging out of this confection, as the body lowered itself from the windowsill, was the other boy, Pierre. She gave herself the advice she had eventually got from Father Muller to make a distinction between fantasy and reality and to check what her desire led her to believe. She would have liked to believe that this was a giant chrysalis at the moment of becoming a butterfly.

She watched in fascination as the other boy eventually lowered himself on to the courtyard. Pierre was now standing in the full-length evening dress she recognised as one which her daughter Esmeralda had worn to a dance on Old Year's night for her debut. It had been relegated to a trunk of old clothes which Emilia hoped would one day become the dressing-up box when her grandchildren came to stay. Well, it seemed it had already come into use as a masquerade. Guillaume seemed naked next to Pierre, in just his shorts, as she saw them disappear into the orchid house. Not having Carlos to talk to, she remembered what he had said when she had told him about them covered with chicken feathers. The boy was unsure of who he is. She wanted to creep down and peep at them more closely and see what they were doing, but that felt incorrect, so she decided to return to her own siesta and leave the garden to the children.

The garden, left to the children at siesta, was alive with the plaintive cry of the cigale singing for rain. In the intervals of that lamentation, the garden was a continual moan of the doves. The season was just itself changing its dress from the dry season into the wet season and the pouis and immortelles had dropped their dresses to the ground where the yellow and orange petals ringed the trees. The wide umbrella of branches of the flamboyant trees drenched in red and yellow were like the crinolined skirts prepared for a drag queen's ball.

In the shadows of the orchid house, in the cool of its shade, Pierre danced the dance of the seven veils he had seen Rita Hayworth dance in the film *Salome* discarding her various skirts as Guillaume looked on bewildered, but unmistakably attracted to his friend whom he held in his arms at the discarding of the last veil as he swooned. At that moment he kissed him on the mouth.

'Gawd, is that what it's like to be a girl?'

'Boy, I don't know.'

The boys stood almost naked in front of each other, laughing.

7
The Parish Priest

So, as well as the daily masses, the nuns' confessions, the confessions of the laity, benediction, visits to the sick and dying, Father Muller had on top of all his priestly work, his works of mercy, the momentous funeral of Carlos Calderon, the architect of San Fernando who had built the church, the town hall, the technical college, the boys' college and the extension to the convent for the nuns of Cluny. The town was a monument to the man who loved to sit in his orchid house and clean the leaves of his orchids with an old toothbrush while he smoked his cigarettes.

But on this day of days, Father Muller had time in between everything else, like carrying communion for old Mrs Espinet on Penitence Hill, to escape to Rushworth Street for his weekly visit to Mistress Redhead.

He entered her backyard through a gate cut into the blue galvanise fence which led past the soursop trees and the fowls and ducks which Mistress Redhead had running about and feeding on scraps. He entered the clacking yard and climbed the broken-down backstairs onto the back verandah where she always met him dressed in her housecoat all ready, so as not to waste any time.

'Elizabeth.' Here he allowed himself to call her by her first name, never in the parish, always then, Mistress Redhead.

'Hans.' She dropped the Father Muller and allowed him to kiss her on the cheek while still on the open back verandah, the yard shaded by the almond trees from the road.

Entering the house out of the blinding sun and oppressive humidity of the wet season was like entering a dark and soothing cave, which felt like velvet and shimmered with the watery satin and taffeta antimacassars on Mistress Redhead's proudly upholstered chairs and couch. The curtains were drawn and orange lamps lit up the darkness as they both entered Mistress Redhead's small bedroom with the big brass bed and the varnished bureau. Here they were both in another world. 'I say you not coming today.'

'You know I had to come. How could I not come? You know, the delay with the visits to the sick and…'

'Well, you here now, come, let me take you things.'

You could say that this rendezvous had grown out of the spiritual talks Father Muller had had to give Mistress Redhead when she came to confession with the worry of what she wanted to do to her husband in revenge for going with those girls who hung over the balcony of Chen's shop at the corner of Mucurapo and Coffee Street, or, the revenge when she desired to avenge her people's history with the killing of Mistress Calderon; something her grandfather did not do.

Father Muller was a white man, one of those missionaries, and though Mistress Redhead knew it contradicted everything she thought about white people on the morne, she could not now resist this man who had offered her so much spiritual comfort and had not even thought to ask for any of this which she now gave him, in the arms of her soft and perfumed body. It first happened on the night they had to clear up after the harvest festival and he had dropped her off at home with the remainder of the prizes for the bran tub and hoop-la. He had come in for a little drink of mauby, which was her speciality, and then she gave him one of her finest rums, and one thing led to another and he ended up spending the night and being late for the five o'clock mass.

Life was good to them because it never occurred to Mistress Redhead that these visits, these moments in the cool shadows of her bedroom, were nails to be driven into the saviour. And though it wasn't long before rumour spun out a tale to keep all the ladies and the gentlemen of the parish astonished, Father Muller continued to come through the gate in the blue galvanise fence, through the back yard with the ducks and fowls, to comfort Mistress Redhead and to indulge an acknowledged weakness in himself which had grown out of his loneliness.

Before he left that morning it was on Mistress Redhead's mind to ask him what he thought of play-play girls. Did they really exist? But she decided against it, putting the thought out of her mind, allowing the flavour of their mutual indulgence to linger. Then a thought crept into Mistress Redhead's head. If Hans could leave his priesthood for her, he might, like Eldridge, leave it for them girls or boy-girls on Chen's balcony.

8
The Architect's Widow

And, in a similar way, Emilia Calderon indulged a weakness of hers to believe that her daydreams were true. She continued to live in the big house at the summit of the morne on her own with Justine who had now drawn completely the curtains of her cataracts, so that her big ears, which sprouted hairs, were her only real line of communication to the world around her as she used to say, 'Is only these I have now,' cupping her ears to press them towards where she heard her companions speaking to her.

But Emilia's daydreams were suddenly shattered when she realised that the boy whom she saw as wet as a deer and who at times floated up to her windowsill was Lal the yard boy, and the young girl with whom he did unspeakable things, was her niece, Yvonne.

While the little boys continued to emerge out of Justine's loft stuck with feathers, or in Rita Hayworth get-ups, her niece was having a dangerous liaison with the yard boy. Yes, the sin of impurity was definitely a nail in the cross through the hands and feet of the saviour. But the real danger for Emilia with the liaison was the miscegenation; this young brown deer, wet and trembling, "tupping" her fair niece; "tupping" one of those words, which astonished Father Muller, made him think that Emilia Calderon had something in common with Mistress Redhead's imagination and flight with words.

When she turned to her prie-dieu to kneel and speak to the Little Flower, it seemed to be a daydream after all. Prayer had worked this time. Or, had it?

Still, the next day, the young wet deer came floating up to her window from the garden into her bed, his hot breath with the scent of guavas on her neck, and following stealthily, the young girl to cradle herself in her arms, bringing that other desire.

9
Justine's Last Words

Justine thought that her cataracts were a blessing in disguise. Whatever life had dealt her she thought of as a blessing. It was her nature. But her ears burnt, not with words spoken about her, she had been long forgotten, shuffling around in alpagats while younger women came to do the housework, but with the screams of delight which came from her madam's bedroom at siesta time. She thought maybe she had imagined the death of the master, Carlos Calderon. Was he not buried in Paradise cemetery?

Well, maybe even those cries of delight which she heard at siesta time coming from her madam's bedroom were not nails to be driven into the hands and feet of the saviour, but a sign of the freeing of her madam's larynx. She no longer carried, she noticed, that look of distress on her face.

'Is time I dead, yes,' she said. 'I swear it. I swear point blank upon a pitch-pine board. I swear, I swear. Yea, Lord.' Then, she laughed out loud, her mending falling to the ground, her blind eyes watering with her joy.

The children had loved to hear her swear in this way in her Barbadian accent, which she had lost a little with her journey to Trinidad. They would cry out, 'Say it again, Nurse!' But that time had gone with the girls growing up, getting married and leaving. They were not her girls anymore. Justine was no longer the nurse who could see the excitement and enjoy the cries of her madam's daughters at play.

These tales were first heard in the quiet tones of the confessional, in the gossip on the pews of the parish church, through the whisperings in a secret garden and in the dimly lit bedroom of illicit lovers behind the Radio City cinema near Paradise cemetery. They were heard from an old woman as she looked out from a courtyard above the sea. They were heard while, for some, their childhood disappeared, their youth bewildered them, and their middle age filled them with doubt and then joy. For others, their loneliness filled them with desire, and in their old age they were prepared for death, as a welcome relief from the darkness of cataracts and the discomfort of burning ears.

Ash on Guavas

'This is a darling of an island.' Fitzroy Cuthbert spoke softly to himself as he fumbled with his boots sitting on the verandah of his small board house in the pearly grey of the foreday morning. The moon was bone white. 'Yes, darling,' he smiled, taking up his white enamel mug with the blue rim from the ledge of the verandah and sipping his black coffee. He packed a cigarette, tock, tock, and lit it. He inhaled deeply and sighed. 'Yes. Watch you rise.' He spoke to the island as he saw the first glimmer of pink begin to grow in the sky over Mosquito Ghaut. The night noise of insects began to fade with the encroaching day. This was his sign to collect his fork, spade and hoe from under the house in order to make his daily journey to his farm in the hill above Gages. 'My paradise, here I come. By the sweat of my brow. Today I plant cassava. Tomorrow is bananas.'

Sarah Garnet, his granddaughter, sixteen years old, heard him leave the house. While lying in her bed under the net, the other side of the verandah wall, she felt comforted by his waking; and saw in her mind's eye his climb up the red dirt road into the steadily increasing green of the hills. The hot sun did not take long to rise. Her heart was full of pride. For him, her grandpappy! But her lying in on the first day of the long school vacation was soon shattered by her grand-mother who always rose after her husband: 'Rock of ages cleft for me.' Sarah knew the verses well. She would focus on particular words. Cleft.

'That man is my cross, yes.' Ethel Cuthbert quarrelled and prayed. 'That confounded cigarette', as she opened up the jalousies of her drawing room and threw open the shutters for the day to enter, remembering what the doctor had said about her husband's heart, how the continual smoking was tightening up his arteries. 'What Doctor Simmons know about that man's heart? I could tell him some things about it. What could burst his heart?' Sarah Garnet smiled at her grandmother talking to herself, thinking that she was alone with the old love that she had to be so careful with, before it get suddenly taken away and she get leave in this house alone. 'Let me hide myself in thee.' She had a gospel voice. 'Sarah, child, you up?' A cock crowed in the neighbour's yard.

'Coming, Grandma. Soon.' She knew she still had a few more verses to doze through. And she had her own dreams.

'From thy riven side which flowed.'

Riven. That was another word.

All along the coast the sea breeze rolled the arrowing sugarcane fields, coming up from Mesopotamia and Egypt, past the village of Felicity, where the old sugar mill squatted in the folds of the fields.

Sarah dozed and dreamed. It was Mr Courtney Hunt, her school teacher's voice in the geography lesson on the last day of term. 'And then we had our archipelago. These very islands, an underwater cordillera rose from the sea, exploding with a fire which was the beginning of the world.' Sarah drew her map. It was like a bow stretched out into the Atlantic Ocean between the eagle's beak of Florida and the iguana of the Venezuelan coast line. Mr Hunt had a poetry for it. That was what made Geography so exciting. With his deep voice, he fed her words while she drew. 'See the rosary of islands, the splintered arc. See each mountain peak; an indigo, green serration which runs along the rim of the new world basin.' He spoke, almost in pentameters. He had a cane which traced the archipelago on a glossy map which hung on the classroom wall. Sarah drew, absorbed, to the tap of the cane.

Then, Antonina Markham spoilt it. Poking Sarah in the ribs under the desk, she giggled, 'He too sweet eh? You don't think? That deep voice of his. He's a honey.'

'Shush,' Sarah had whispered, concentrating on the lecture and her drawing.

'Not the labours of my hands…Sarah, Sarah, child. Them lilies and ferns need water before the hot sun reach them.' Sarah awoke from her reverie into her grandmother's poetry, her daily demands and chores. The flavours of her grandmother's cooking had dispelled her grandfather's coffee and tobacco smoke. The lilies yielded their own perfume as she watered them from the watering can in the corner.

'I going into the mountain today, Sarah, to meet your grandpappy.' Ethel Cuthbert stood at her kitchen sink washing and cutting vegetables which she was putting on to boil for a broth. 'That is what Dr Simmons say. Give him fresh vegetables, no ground provision, cut out the starch. Plenty carrots, greens, string beans and spinach. He must think the man is a horse or what, that he only want to be eating grass. Dr Simmons don't know a strong man working on his land need some beef, something to fill his belly?' Ethel Cuthbert was staring out of her kitchen window at the mountain she would soon climb.

'Let me come with you Grandma. You going walking alone

in this hot sun, and you yourself have pressure.'

'Oh, so young people come like parents to their grandparents now? Girl, I walking up that mountain since I is your age. That is a natural place for me to be. You stay here. Sweep the yard. And you have study to do? Something you writing for Mr Courtney Hunt?' She raised her eyebrows. 'I don't have to remind you why your mother have you in the school.'

Yes, Sarah knew that she was eager to get down to Mr Courtney Hunt's essay: The Origins of the Archipelago.

The sun was up now. It was a hot day. Sarah gazed from the verandah out over the savannah where the goats were tethered. The guava trees were yellow and green with fruit. She could see over to Fort Ghaut and Spring Ghaut. The green of the island was like jade. It glinted. The sea was cobalt. The sky vivid. Indigo. Mr Courtney Hunt's word.

'Sarah, I going now, child.' Ethel Cuthbert met with Sarah in the yard where she was watering the purple and white impatiens flowers she had planted to please her grandmother along the gravel path that led up to the front steps of the board house. She had put conches and shells from the beach at Endeavour's Rest all along the border when she was a little girl, singing her rhyme: 'Mary, Mary quite contrary, how does your garden grow? With silver bells and cockle shells and pretty maids all in a row.'

'Come, give your grandmother a kiss.' Ethel Cuthbert proffered her cheek. Then she took Sarah's chin in her bony fingers, staring into her eyes. 'You is a sweet child. God knows how you mother could leave you with me and go off into the world yonder. And your father, well!' Ethel Cuthbert jerked her head with derision in the direction where she thought Miami was, as if it was just up the road. 'Christina must think that American dollars is everything.' Ethel Cuthbert picked up her bundle from the bottom step. 'I have a nice broth for Grandpappy. Some for you on the stove. Keep yourself good. Don't be eating too many of them green guavas and get belly ache. Look for we sun down.'

Sarah stared at her grandmother's back as she climbed the red dirt road towards the hills. She continued to stare till her pale yellow dress was part of the light, till her gospel voice had faded: 'Nothing in my hand I bring; Simply to thy cross I cling. Naked, come to thee for dress…'

Sarah mused: cleft, riven, naked, cling.

She went to her small desk with the inkwell where she had her books covered in brown paper with her name and subjects written with a broad fountain pen nib in royal blue Quink ink. Sarah Garnet, Geography, Salem Government School. She wrote in her copy book, choosing her words carefully from her list of definitions. She drew the wall of the volcano between the mountains. From the crater she drew a narrow margin as the main vent into the magma chamber. In cascading squiggles she built up the dome of her illustrated volcano for her essay, The Origins of the Archipelago. She coloured the molten lava spilling over the rim. Mushrooming above her crater was a grey-black ash cloud.

The day seemed to be flying by without Sarah noticing.

Then Sarah felt that it had gone strangely quiet. The birds were not singing. Suddenly, there was a roar, like that of two 747 jets low above the house. Then she heard Antonina Markham shouting, 'Sarah, Sarah, come outside and see.'

Sarah dropped her pen, slammed down her copy book and ran out to the verandah. 'Sarah, watch, Soufriere! Watch the mountain!'

Sarah and Antonina stood clinging to each other and staring at the ash cloud belch from the crater on the summit of the Soufriere Hills. They watched the column of ash cloud move with the wind off the Atlantic. It was moving towards them and their village.

'Go inside your house girl.' Antonina cried to Sarah as she turned to run down the road to her own home. 'Read your Bible.'

Sarah sat in her grandmother's tidy drawing room on one of her varnished Morris chairs by the small table with the lace doily and the green cut-glass vase with her new yellow and red plastic flowers. She rocked gently back and forth and sang her grandmother's hymn. 'Rock of ages cleft for me. Let me hide myself in thee.' She thought she could hear her singing in the house, she thought she could hear her cajoling her grandpappy. She felt helpless, not knowing what to do, the words of the hymn cushioning her.

It had grown dark. She switched on the light that hung in a white-clouded glass shade from the centre of the ceiling.

On the wind that reached the hill village there was the sulphur smell of rotten eggs. Sarah closed the verandah door and pulled in the shutters after lowering the jalousies. She stuffed newspaper in the crevices of the doors and windows.

Outside was like night. The street lights had been turned on.

There was another roar and then a scream. From the window she saw the Gages wall rip open. She ran down the steps into the yard to pick up the washing off the line. Ethel Cuthbert's best sheets. By the time she reached back upstairs, it had begun to fall like hard rain. Inside, it sounded like a bucket of nails falling on the galvanised roof. She remembered Mr Courtney Hunt describe the pumice stones falling. He had read to them from Pliny the Younger, about the cinders thicker and hotter the nearer he approached, the pumice stone blackened, scorched and cracked by the fire. She remembered the date, August 79 AD in the Bay of Naples. It sounded so pretty. Pompeii.

When Sarah looked out of the window she could not see the orange street lights. She sat under the ceiling bulb and rocked herself. She shut her eyes. Then, the lights went out.

The hillside above the green banana valley opened up in her mind. Her grandpappy, Fitzroy Cuthbert, was in his cassava patch weeding and hoeing, a half-finished cigarette was placed behind his ear. Sitting under a cashew tree in her pale yellow dress was her grandma Ethel Cuthbert pouring vegetable broth into a white enamel bowl. Sarah felt safe in her thoughts and prayers for her grandparents' safety.

'Sarah.' It was Mr Courtney Hunt's deep voice in her head. 'I come for you. You know I would come for you. The helicopter is waiting outside. Didn't you hear the roar of its propellers?' Soon, they were above the island, the sea like rippling galvanised sheeting. The small farms and villages higgledy piggledy. The sun was hidden by the ash cloud. They were veering towards Galway. Over Harris and Webbs. 'Look, Sarah. See the pyroclastic flow. See it moving down Belham River valley. See, it takes everything in its way. More than one hundred miles an hour, more than 800 degrees Celsius. See the wonder that made the archipelago.'

When Sarah roused herself she was still humming and rocking. Like days had passed.

'Miss Garnet, open up, open up.' It was a man's voice she did not know. Sarah opened the front door slowly. The floor and ledges of the verandah were covered with grey sand. Ash. There was a small pickup truck in the road with its lights on. There was the smell of gunpowder in the still air. Everything was muffled. 'This is bad news child, come.' The man was wearing an ash mask. She remembered the evacuation procedures they had once learnt at school, how to put on the ash masks.

'The Lord has taken them into himself.' A woman she recognised as a friend of her grandmother's put her arms around her shoulder. 'Don't show the child.'

Sarah looked instinctively to the back of the pickup truck. She heard the sound of a zip tearing through plastic.

'Is OK,' she said. 'I know about these things. I've studied the nature of these things.'

Two men then lowered onto the ground the two stretchers from the back of the pickup with the black plastic body bags. The corpses lay on their backs with their arms across their chests.

'They would have become like charred wood.' Sarah said. She turned to the small group of people who had collected and whom she now recognised even in their ash masks. 'You see, if the pyroclastic flow seize you. Your clothes go catch on fire, your hair will just go, just so, disappear. As you breathe in that air, your lungs will haemorrhage. Your lung tissue will carbonise.' The increasing crowd listened to the young girl, who, as she talked, from time to time stared at what were the corpses of her grandparents, Fitzroy and Ethel Cuthbert. They were like charred wood. She noticed that their knees were slightly bent.

Two weeks later, the evacuation had begun. The road from Plymouth to Salem was a long line of evacuees. On the backs of trucks and carts people carried all that they possessed: tables, chairs, cabinets, fridges, stoves, boxes, suitcases, chickens and rabbits in coops. A boy carried a parrot on his arm. Goats and donkeys tethered to carts, trotted with the slowly moving procession along the coastal road. The wind was in the faces of men, women and children. All trudged, breathing heavily in their ash masks. They had lost everything. The grey waves crashed on the shore with relentless monotony. The light was ash, ash covered every withered tree and all the ground.

'You must go Sarah. You must go. For your education. It's all arranged. Some of our own people will meet you. We who remain will fight for the reclamation of the place we know and love as home.'

'Come with me.' Sarah touched Mr Courtney Hunt's arm. She had never done that before. Only then she thought, he can't be that much older. Older yes, but not that much older.

Alongside the ship, out in the harbour, as Sarah mounted the steps to the deck, Courtney Hunt pointed out the name of the ship emblazoned on her bow, HMS Liverpool. History continues to echo and re-echo its story, she thought, remembering her history lessons on the West Indians of that city of Liverpool. She hoped her passage and arrival would be different.

From the deck, Sarah waved to Courtney Hunt in the returning ferry. Beyond, she saw her 'darling' of an island as Fitzroy Cuthbert, her grandpappy, called it each morning before his climb into the fertile slopes below the Soufriere Hills as he fumbled with his boots on the verandah, drank black coffee and smoked that 'confounded cigarette' as Ethel Cuthbert used to call it. Sarah hummed, 'Let me hide myself in thee.'

From her pocket, Sarah took out a guava which she had picked from the tree in her yard before leaving home, not forgetting to wash off the ash and scrub it in soap and water. She bit into the fruit and let the green tang of her island burst in her mouth as she inhaled the fragrance of guavas.

The Archbishop's Egg

Archbishop Sorzano was up even earlier than usual. As he opened one half of the shutters and lifted the jalousies of the other in the bedroom of his palace, he noticed, in the still moonlight of what was almost dawn, that the African tulip tree in the yard had bloomed. It confirmed his belief in miracles and in the certainty of what he was now planning this foreday morning.

It was the Saturday before the first Sunday of Advent and he felt a definite expectation in the early morning air; the beginning of something, an idea. Something was hatching, as Mrs Goveia, his housekeeper would say, 'Your Grace, I have a feeling something really hatching here.' Something was coming. After all, this was Advent, oui!

The island was on a cusp. The island was also in a crisis. Something had to change. Wet season was finishing, dry season about to come. The wide green Caroni Plain which grew out of the swamps, the oyster beds and the old rice fields, was no longer arrowing with sugarcane flowers, but no matter, hope would come from elsewhere. Crop time, that was something of the past; there would have to be another kind of harvest.

This was how the Archbishop's mind first played with his fantasy and his idea when he used to jog along over the potholed roads in his little Mazda, a gift from his old parish, until he hit the newly asphalted six-lane highway into the capital, which Ronald Parsons, the new Prime Minister, a sort of jack-in-the-box character who had just jumped up out of nowhere seizing upon the idea, an election winner, to reject the original twin names of the Western leaders of the second world war, Churchill and Roosevelt, calling it the Eric Williams, the Father of the Nation Highway. Ronald Parsons was of the mind that he might bask in the glory of that pioneer, Dr Eric Williams. It blazed a trail between light industry, new suburbs and the rotting sugarcane fields. The break-down hoarding, proclaiming the re-christening, was once adorned with humming birds, scarlet ibis and chaconias in iridescent reds, greens and yellows, and had stood competing with 'Welcome Home Brian Lara' and 'Drink Carib Beer', well out of date and falling down under a collapsed electricity pole, draped dangerously with high-powered electric cables. All the colours of the hoarding were now fading, washed out in the rainy season. Something new was needed to clean up this country, the Archbishop thought.

What exactly would turn out Archbishop Sorzano was not too sure, but he had the idea to make things new. The country needed sprucing up. People needed hope. He liked to think of it as an inspiration. The Holy Spirit had sent it. It was a revelation even, now that he thought about it further. The very first inkling of the idea had come to him just after the consecration at the early morning mass. Only Mrs Goveia was there serving his mass, and he remembered that he was distracted by her unorthodox way of sitting back on her legs while kneeling and ringing the bell at the consecration. Things had really changed since he was a boy.

Archbishop Sorzano picked up his iPhone, a present from Ronald Parsons, one of the many presents and gifts of money out of his own pocket the Prime Minister gifted to his constituents, and walked out onto the balcony of his palace overlooking the Savannah. 'Ronny.'

'Boy, you up early, Your Grace. You become an ascetic in your Archbishop days?'

'Where you? Sound like rain falling by you up in the valley. It dry down here.'

'In the shower, boy.'

'In the shower? What? You in that new gym you build for yourself in your new house. You is something else, yes. I'm amazed I can get in touch with you so quickly. Like prayer, like a direct line to God the Father at any moment.'

'You calling me God now, and Father?'

And I see you call yourself Father of the Nation after the Doc, bestowing gratis everywhere.'

'On call at a moment's notice. Be prepared was our motto, remember Scouts under Father Knox-by-Night, St Mary's Down-the-Islands. Sea Scouts.'

'Our first navy, boy. You remember that, and Father Knox-by-Day, that white priest.'

'Them jokes in them days. And look at me now. Commander-in-Chief. Who would think that?'

The Archbishop smiled. Ronny was still a schoolboy at heart, a wicked naivety was expressed in his smile. He was always acting as if he had gone to drama school. It was Mrs Goveia again who had underlined it the day after the election. 'Ronald Parsons, Prime Minister? Lord save my people!' What he had told the interviewer on the television was that he was the right person at the right time in the right place. 'He is the wrong person in the wrong place at the wrong time,' Mrs Goveia spat out as she got up and walked out of the room and went to pray for the salvation of her people. 'Sweet Sacrament Divine…' she wailed as she went down into the kitchen with her favourite hymn.

'Just an overgrown schoolboy,' the Archbishop had called after her, humouring the woman and his school pardner, Ronny. They had played football together. They had played cricket. He remembered Intercol: 'Saint Mary's we want a goal! QRC we want a goal!' Those chants had stirred the young fellas in those days, and then the country had eventually reached the World Cup. Soca Warriors was the cry. All that had faded now, football and football money had been the pot of gold then to dip into for the gifts shared out. Now they needed something else to carry them further, now that Ronald Parsons was the Prime Minister and Louis Sorzano was the Archbishop.

Everyone must hear about his idea in time, the Archbishop thought, young and old, man and woman. People would soon be tweeting and posting it on Facebook from all parts of the island, from Gran Couva to Galeota, from Manzanilla to Maracas. They would soon be twittering to each other, he smiled to himself; the birds in the African tulip tree amusing him, messaging each other from island to island, Chaguanas to Crown Point, Palo Seco to Parlatuvier with the news. They would get it instantly while driving in a car, walking down the road, in a taxi, in a maxi-taxi, on the beach, in a bus on the Priority, up a tree, on a donkey cart, by the standpipe, in the lavatory, or in the shower, like the Prime Minister himself.

Ronny Parsons had seduced his holy friend the Archbishop to come that last night of the election campaign to Woodford Square, in the very university of the Doc, to endorse his candidature. The Archbishop thought now that he was owed something in return.

Even then, Ronald Parsons had wondered what his friend the Archbishop would be asking of him in return, and the

Archbishop wondered to what more he might be compromised into giving his imprimatur. Highways, archiepiscopal endorsements were one thing, but what else? What about dignity and decency? Ronny said he would clean up the corruption, jail the drug traffickers, reach up in America to bring back criminals. He would search them out in high places. Sweep the yard clean. Put back God in his place. Sometimes Archbishop Sorzano wondered if Ronny wanted to be an archbishop himself, if he wanted to be Jesus Christ, the way he dispensed out of his own pocket largesse to his constituents, feeding the thousands, as it were, with a loaf of bread and a few fishes, though it was more than a loaf of bread and a few fishes that Ronny had his hands on. It worried him how he was speaking more and more like one of those evangelical preachers at a revivalist meeting, all that gesticulation. He was a real actor. There were even rumours that Ronny wanted to found a church and have his own priests.

They had had the ideals when they were Scouts and boys in the CYO and Legion of Mary. Now they had bigger visions. The Archbishop hoped that his vision would woo the Prime Minister.

'Ronny, done with your stupidness. Turn off that shower in your fancy gym. I have a proposal which will suit both of us. Kill two birds with one stone. A miracle has occurred.'

'What you saying?'

'Miracle, a miraculous apparition has taken place. I have recently had notice of it from one of my country parish priests. And this thing, if I don't channel it properly, we might miss an opportunity. We have to work together.'

'You mean, put the lid on it, in case scandal come to the church. You know is enough scandal we have these days. The abuse of children, buller man as priest, and the population only feeling encouraged in this gay rights thing. And I know I mustn't confuse the abuse with the gay thing, like them Russians and them African leaders, all kind of leaders. But what happen to all you, in truth.'

'No, Ronny, leave those regrettable errors of a few. You know I won't tolerate that nastiness in my church. Just like you should not tolerate it in the country, no matter what is happening elsewhere. And, gay rights? No. Keep the old laws. Mother England give them up, but you must keep them. But as the gospel says, don't put your light under a bushel. Come out hard, so to speak. Don't let the UN confuse your mind with human rights etc.'

'Well, somebody must have a bushel, or whatever you call it, well clamp down on it, because I ent hear of nothing like a miracle take place. The papers don't have nothing. My fellas haven't reported nothing. I know this new Pope trying a PR thing. I've not picked up no miracle on Twitter.'

'That is it Ronny. Is a secret. I have the parish priest under wraps about this thing. You know how it could cause parish rivalry and so on, Charismatics against Opus Dei. History does tell you you must watch them Jesuits. But give the new Pope a chance, eh. We have to see what he go really do.'

'But what you want me to do with a miracle that nobody know nothing about?'

'That's just it, we going to tell them.'

'And what is the two birds we going to kill with this one stone?'

'Think of it Ronny. Is birds you talking about? That is the right train of thought. Tweet tweet.' The Archbishop laughed out loud.

'Louis, who don't know about Twitter? You come late to this thing.'

'Is not know, is use for a purpose. Is true. I hear even the Queen of England tweeting now. Good thing, because if she find a man in she bedroom again, she will be able to alert security one time.'

'You is Sparrow now, you singing calypso,' Ronny Parsons chortled down the phone.

Archbishop Sorzano's brain was more than hatching the idea he had woken with that morning as he stood on the balcony of his palace watching the sun get brighter and dry up the dew on the grass below the African tulip tree, while the Prime Minister was towelling his wet body in his gym. 'Think of it Ronny.'

'Louis, stop holding me in suspense. I have to prepare for a Cabinet meeting.'

'Boy, this is the idea that your Cabinet will want to discuss.'

'What's that? A miracle, a miraculous apparition? And, anyway, who it is appear? Who making the apparition? What we need is a Saudi Arab to appear on the world stage and jack up the oil prices even further like in the eighties. Stop all that Sunni Shia stupidness. Make a true Hosay of oil and gas hikes so we could really beat some tassa for truth. Who you say?'

'The Blessed Virgin Mary, of course, who else does appear miraculously? You think we're not people like other people in Italy, Portugal, France and Spain, or like our neighbour Venezuela. Even Chavez, when he was alive, profit from that you know. You forget the Madonna of Koromoto, the Madonna of Betania. You think we're not people like how it was in war-torn Bosnia where our own people went on pilgrimage to Medjugorje in Herzegovina. Our people need solace and comfort too. Boy they need it too bad with the killing that going on. When you go stop this thing? You haven't brought that to a stop yet. Everyday, everyday. And I hear you tell the people you can't change water into wine. In fact I hear you say, not yet. Is so? They go run you out of office if you tongue runaway with you, you know.'

'Louis, I not going to have any criticism of the government by the Archbishop, or by the Church. All you must remember you here longer than we and I ent see all you change anything in any big way. In fact, all you have a lot to change as I tell you already, before you come telling government to change. Not now. I have no time when I'm preparing my first budget.'

'That's just it. Budget. This has a bearing on your very same budget.'

'Look, Archbishop, speak to me later. Duty calls. I go see you boy.'

Mrs Goveia would be an agent in this business, a messenger from heaven, an agent provocateur. 'Mrs Goveia?'

'Your Grace?' She never called him Louis since the sealed letter from Rome had arrived with the announcement of his appointment. 'Your Grace?' Sometimes he had to prevent her from collapsing on her knees and taking his hand to kiss his ring of office.

'Mrs Goveia, just bring that new iPhone here a moment.'

'Where it is, Your Grace?'

'It's on my prie-dieu with my breviary.'

'Here's your Ronald Parsons' opportunity.' Mrs Goveia put the phone down on the breakfast table.

'Well, I want you to use it. Phone the *Express* newspapers. He pressed down his bejewelled finger. 'Now, you'll repeat what I say, and no more. No embroidery.'

Mrs Goveia obeyed her Archbishop. She spoke to the newspaper's office. 'I have something to report. Yes, report. A miraculous apparition of the Blessed Virgin Mary has taken place in the parish of Gran Couva. Yes. You hear what I say. Is what I telling you. What? You can't spell apparition. Look that up later. Google it, nuh. Take it shorthand, dictaphone, or whatever you use today. You want me email? Who she appear to? That not come out yet. You have to wait for next report. My name? You fast. Is anonymous. Say a devout anonymous.'

'Well done, Mrs Goveia.'

'Who is that with me? I say, you too fast.' Mrs Goveia handed the phone to the Archbishop. 'Your Grace, what is the meaning of this?'

'You don't need to know more than I've told you. I don't want you talking to nobody about it.'

'But you just make me tell it to the papers.'

'It's up to them to get the details. They never like to do any real investigation, they too 'fraid.'

'When this take place? Your Grace?'

'The less you know, the better, at the moment, Mrs Goveia.'

The news spread like how big cane-fire crop time used to spread from field to field. Mrs Goveia's report had been conjured into a multiplicity of headlines in all the papers and news bulletins on the radio stations and on the TV. Mrs Goveia was instructed to say: 'No comment. The Archbishop is looking into the matter.'

But, in Gran Couva, it was something else. The parish priest could not cope with the calls, and the church was filling up. People were awaiting something. Not that anyone knew at that stage who really appear to whom, or where the apparition had even taken place, certainly not the new parish priest Father Fortune. His best bet was to keep the rosary going. Collection boxes were filling up, and already votive candles had sold out.

By the next afternoon, a pilgrimage was making its way up

to Gran Couva; a cavalcade of cars from all parts of the island, but also people on foot, on bicycle, motorbike, donkey cart. And then, later that evening, the ominous whirring of a helicopter. Someone shout out, 'Is Ronald Parsons!'

People made a clearing for it on the cricket ground in the middle of Gran Couva, which was encircled with lighted deyas as at Diwali time, but the chopper swooped low and then took off again, and circled right over the gulf and headed back for town. The helicopter itself was like an apparition from some kind of sci-fi heaven, twinkling with the stars and the suburban strip beneath the northern hills, the villages scattered on the plain; like the firmament had fallen down, the Milky Way twinkling along the Eastern Main Road, from Laventille to Arima.

People start to shout that they reconnoitring the area to see the apparition coming down from heaven; security forces searching the heavens. 'Watch out boy.'

In the morning papers it was reported that not only had children seen the Virgin Mary, but she had also appeared to some of the women of the parish, and one had claimed to be healed from a fresh cold, another from hard of hearing, and yet another had loosed her tongue, like in the gospels; healing was taking place and others were speaking in tongues. Hallelujah was the cry.

Two days later: the budget announcement had been postponed.

The Prime Minister called the Archbishop when he got the morning papers.

'Louis, this thing out of hand.'

'I haven't yet seen the papers, Ronny. Blood, you say.'

'They say, she weeping blood. I get that on Facebook where they have all kind of story and pics. Even a photograph claiming to be a true image and likeness of the Virgin Mary herself. Not to mention what the bloggers are saying.'

'These things happen Ronny, stuff happens, even in Italy, that big football country. This is what we had wanted. This is how we go kill the two birds with the one stone. We go tweet weself about the world; it go be like the time of Soca Warriors, but this time is a bigger game, a supernatural one.'

'This thing go make us a laughing stock in the world. I have to go and speak to the UN next month.'

'Ronny, watch the signs of the times. Your budget get postpone. Well, we have to have a budget. We have to deal with the recession. And it will be better when we have some real money to talk about. Hindu and Muslim fundamentalist prayer meeting shut down. Nobody gone. That American preacher, the one who cry on the TV because they find him with a prostitute, he not coming again in the stadium. They say the churches emptying all over the island and is one steady stream to Gran Couva, a simple little village in central. Like Bethlehem, you remember Bethlehem? Is how things used to be long ago with the big Corpus Christi procession. This is we Pagwa, we Diwali and Hosay all roll into one big revival jamboree. You should be pleased the way you only supporting the Indians and them. We thing coming back. And it truly ecumenical, because I only hearing Hallelujah and Shanti Shanti and Om and Shalom, every kind of religious chant and mantra as people going up to Gran Couva. People feel is prayer go change things. Every kind of drum in this country beating. I believe they have imam and pundit, Orisha archbishop. All of them in the procession trying to get in on the thing. I hear they want to bring David Rudder back from Canada to sing *High Mas*. I've decided to lead the recitation of the rosary there this afternoon, like long-time Laventille devotions. What about coming? You could come by helicopter. And you have a private one?'

'Not me in this confusion. The government is staying out of it, except to send police and members of the armed forces. You know how them Muslimeen is still a threat, and now all the drug lords with their gangs themselves. We don't want a next takeover, like in '90. And we still need to catch them ganja smokers up in central. All you think is incense you burning up there? Watch the sign of the times, Louis.'

By the end of the week the story had spread across the world. Those gone mad on their Blackberries were telling the tale of the Black Madonna of Gran Couva who was reported weeping and sweating blood. And it wasn't children or women, or even Catholics, but a Rasta fella from Erin who decided to break into the church on the run, and startled by what he saw, then ran out and called the people on the road to Gran Couva.

Archbishop Sorzano sent his vicar-general from the cathedral to take specimens to send to the Holy Office in Rome, to verify the authenticity of blood, sweat and tears. You could already follow the story on the Vatican website, the Twitter feed had it all.

Trinbago was at the centre of things.

Weeks and months, a whole year passed, and still no verdict. But then people were now on regular procession and pilgrimage, texting as they went. *Time* magazine and *Newsweek* run the story. *Readers Digest* carry something. Trinidad was the place to come on pilgrimage. The national airline suddenly began to make a profit for the first time in its history. Trinidad was a holy place. Never mind Mecca, no need to go to Holy Land, bathe in the Ganges.

Ronny Parsons called one morning the following Christmas.

'This is Archbishop's house...'

He spoke quickly. 'Now, all the hotels sell out and we have cruise ship booking for about six years in advance. People on the move Louis. People on pilgrimage and the treasury is bulging. Is not oil boy, but is money. This go deal with the recession, with insurance and pension bobol and all the other kind a bobol that going on in the parliament, the judiciary, the police, big business, quarrying, deforestation, flooding, all that keeping back this country. See now what you mean. You have your church popular again and we have a chance too, we get away. But the blood thing Louis, I don't think we need to emphasise the weeping and sweating of blood. Let's keep it clean. By the way, there is a request from the Pentecostals, the Hindus and the Muslims, a petition. They want to know why it is we giving the Catholics cheap flight on the airline to come down from America and England for carnival. I tell them is religious tolerance. I tell them is pilgrimage. Have a good Christmas. Come over for pastelles and parang. Like the Messiah really come this year. Not an oil-rich Arab, but a Jewish girl.'

When Archbishop Sorzano returned from the midnight mass, he played the Prime Minister's message and smiled. In the moonlight the African tulip tree had kept on blooming all that year, a tree of flames, a miracle in itself.

Long after all the bookings were secure, and the future looked rosy, the letter from the Holy Office in Rome came back with the verdict that the blood was goat blood, and the tears were heavily chlorinated water with some unidentified bacteria.

But, by that time, Prime Minister Ronny Parsons and Archbishop Louis Sorzano had made a killing, and were forecast to keep on. Their myth had joined all those other myths of miracles and sacred places in other parts of the world. Coffers were full.

But, the cry all over the country was still who thief the people money? And, what going on?

Faith's Pilgrimage

Faith's mother took her away from The Convent of The Holy Child.

'Yes, my dear,' said her mother's sister, Inez, Faith's favourite aunty, on the phone one afternoon soon after: 'You're quite right. She'll be spoilt. Have you heard the other girls, the way they shout and scream and get on? Quite hysterical! Faith is different. She must be saved. Take her away at once.'

'The child is not herself,' Marie Wainwright, Faith's mother, insisted. 'I must get to the bottom of this.'

Mother Philomena of the Five Wounds, in dismay, pronounced in the convent parlour, 'Young girls need order and they need other girls.'

'For what?' Marie Wainwright asked cynically.

Faith was schooled by her mother at home. Her classroom was on the front gallery where her desk was in the corner stacked with brown *Royal Readers*, maths exercises and *The High Roads of History*, telling the story of the Princes in the Tower; terrified little boys hugging themselves on the cold steps of the Tower of London. These pages were left open on the verandah, fluttering in the breeze behind the jalousies. And, there was the small, blue penny catechism which taught her everything about God and his mysteries; about infallibility and transubstantiation, about the seven sacraments, and about the three virtues: faith, hope and charity. More and more words she learnt, like immortality, which extended her vocabulary and her desire for perfection.

Her mother had christened her Faith. She knew another girl called Charity. Clara Mendonza, her best friend, had told her that she knew a family who had triplets. They were called Faith, Hope and Charity. 'Is it true Clara?' Clara Mendonza said it was true, but Faith did not believe her. No, not anymore. Clara was hysterical!

The old, wooden estate house creaked in the heat and buckled with the wind sighing outside in the casaurina trees. Faith's father was already out on his horse on the sugarcane estate. Her brothers and sisters were at school. Faith was alone. The shade of the yard was blood red with the flamboyant.

'Dear God, please don't let my Mummy die.' Since being alone with her mother, without her friends, Faith had got it into her head that her mother was going to die. If she went out and left her on her own in the house, she thought she would not return. The only way to stop this happening was to make a vow.

She knelt under the picture of the Madonna in della Robbia blue with the dried palm from last Palm Sunday stuck behind the frame, scratching the cream wall. This was where they had said the family rosary. Here she vowed that she would be a nun if her mother did not die; vowed it before the picture of the archangels set in battle array around the haloed Madonna. 'Holy Mary, I'll be a nun if you don't let Mummy die.' Faith lay prostrate as she had seen Audrey Hepburn do in *The Nun's Story*.

Then Faith went and stared at her mother from the doorway where she was lying on the bed with her eyes closed, resting after lunch. She could not see her breathing. She tiptoed closer and peered into her mother's face. Then she saw the heaving chest, her breasts rising and subsiding. She heard her mother exhaling. She was alive! Faith whispered 'Mummy' and 'Thank you God' as she backed out of the room, hoping her mother would not suddenly open her eyes and wonder what she was doing, tiptoeing around her bedroom, looking as if she had seen a ghost. But she had to go and look again in half an hour. Still her mother was breathing.

'Faith, is that you again, child? Try and rest.' Marie Wainwright had guessed her daughter's fears. She's no longer a little girl, she thought, seeing Faith's filling-out body under her cotton chemise.

Outside, the cigale cried for rain, sawing its tune in the flamboyant tree which was dropping its red dress on the ground.

'No Clara. No.' Faith heard herself. Why had Clara done that in the linen room? Faith examined herself.

She heard her voice again in the chapel at the convent. She thought of herself as a jug or a vessel being filled with gushing water as from the fountain in the middle of the nuns' cloister. 'Fill me up, fill me up.' The floorboards in her bedroom creaked below her knees, which had found the spot by her bed where she said her morning and night prayers.

There was, too, the injunction to be emptied. Poured out! God, well Jesus, had emptied himself on the cross. 'Empty yourselves,' exhorted Mother Philomena of The Five Wounds in the Marion Hall, all the girls giggling into their hands, whispering and tugging at each other while they passed sweets along the line, hiding their faces behind their lace mantillas.

'Empty me, empty me.' Faith prayed, not really knowing what it meant. But, something special might happen. Maybe the stigmata might spring blood from her hands and feet.

Clara Mendonza giggled, peeping through her fingers while the two girls were kneeling in the chapel.

'Faith, Faith! Fill me up, fill me up! Empty me, empty me!' Afterwards, Clara Mendonza laughed and threw back her head in the playground near the grotto of Our Lady of Lourdes with the little Saint Bernadette. Clara was gulping down her red sweet drink, which spilt on her white bodice as she jumped up as if she was in a carnival band and her song was a calypso, 'Fill me up, fill me up! Empty me, empty me!' She danced across the school yard, her blue pleated uniform skirt caught up too high above her brown knees. Faith joined in, lifting her own skirt and chasing after Clara, fleeing to hide under the Julie mango trees.

'Clara Mendonza, Faith Wainwright!' Mother Philomena of the Five Wounds shouted sternly across the school yard, 'Not a way for devout convent girls to be behaving. Go to the detention room at once.' The detention room was the linen room, where the nuns' white cotton habits hung like ghosts and smelt of vertivert, the cus-cus grass to keep away the moths.

'Faith, Faith! Come and look.' Clara Mendonza hid between the long white habits. Faith tiptoed to find her. Hide and seek.

'No Clara, no, I won't. No Clara, no!'

They said she had fainted and they had found her on the floor.

On this particular afternoon, when she got up from her rest, Faith and her mother were going to go into San Andres; the town, which tumbled down to the gulf, was four miles away from the sugarcane estates. This was the day that Marie Wainwright had to go to her own mother's grave in the cemetery at Le Paradis. Now that Faith was at home from school, she would take the child with her.

'Find the trowel and the little garden fork,' Marie Wainwright called from her bedroom as she got dressed and powdered her nose.

Faith was already in her best party frock, her white organza with the yellow butterflies alighting in the folds of her skirt, and hidden in the puffs of her sleeves. She closed her eyes as her fingers fiddled with the hooks and fasteners at the back, the little pearl buttons down the front. Her dress was too tight. She would not look in the mirror.

'Where is that bus? Broken down again in Barackpore?' Marie Wainwright waited with her daughter at the bottom of the gap where the gravel drive met the hot pitch road at the junction from Mosquito Creek and Fyzabad. 'It's quite ridiculous that you can't get a taxi or a bus at Cross Crossing in the middle of the afternoon.'

Faith had her eyes peeled for a bus in the distance, or a taxi suddenly appearing round the corner from Mucurapo. She carried a straw basket with the trowel and garden fork and a clutch of golden zinnia plants. She didn't like her mother getting upset, particularly in the street with other people watching. She wished, and yes, she prayed, for the bus to arrive quickly.

'Must be a funeral in the country.' Marie Wainwright spoke to herself and her daughter as she watched the shining black hearse, glinting in the hot sun, descend the hill towards where she and Faith were standing. It crept towards them, but they didn't see it being followed by the usual procession. People in the street stopped and stared as people do when a hearse passes by. The woman and her daughter watched it as it approached them. It slowed down completely and then stopped in front of them.

'Mrs Wainwright? Good afternoon.' The chauffeur of the hearse leant out of the window of the cab and spoke politely, smiling. 'It's you, isn't it, Mrs Wainwright? You mustn't stand in this hot sun.' Then he smiled again and looked down at the little girl at her side. 'Your daughter?'

'Oh, of course, Mr Samaroo. Of course it's you. I should've known. Yes of course it's me, and this is Faith. You're quite right.'

'She's a real young girl now.'

Faith blushed.

Then Faith was all eyes; first for Mr Samaroo but then she bowed her head a little shyly. She was looking not at Mr Samaroo in the front cab, but at the length of the hearse behind, at the place where if you saw a hearse you had to look to see what you knew must be there in the shining, brown-varnished coffin mounted high and in full view through the glass windows all around. Why did they have to show it? Why not cover it up? Faith thought.

'No, we're empty, no loved one. I just come from Monkey Town.' Mr Samaroo spoke, looking at Faith and seeing her questions and thoughts written on her open, upturned face. 'There's a lot of space for both of you, Mrs Wainwright, if you would give me the honour to drive with me. You're going into town, yes? There's a big hold up, a bus in a ravine up Diamond way. I know the traces between the cane, so I get through.' Mr Samaroo was getting out of the hearse and was already going around to the door on the other side and opening it gallantly. 'Enter here,' beckoning the mother and daughter to cross to the passenger's side.

It had occurred to Faith that she might have had to be bundled into the back. This was when she was tugging at her mother's dress and keeping her there, rooted to the hot pitch road. 'Let's wait for the bus,' she said, between her clenched teeth.

'Come along dear. It's very kind of Mr Samaroo. We'll all be travelling in one of these one day. Isn't that right Mr Samaroo?' The two grown ups chuckled. The child watched her step.

'Yes Madam. Yes Madam, very amusing,' Mr Samaroo was saying softly as he made sure Faith's pretty white organza didn't get trapped in the door as he pressed it shut softly with a clunk, once Mrs Wainwright was in.

'It's alright dear. Everything will be alright.' Marie Wainwright comforted her daughter's visible distress, while Mr Samaroo crossed back over to the driver's side. 'We'll be in town in a jiffy. No traffic.' Mrs Wainwright patted her daughter on the knee.

Faith sat upright between Mr Samaroo and her mother.

Mr Samaroo overheard the solicitous mother. 'We've got a certain decorum to observe, you know, Madam. So you must excuse if we don't rattle along, even without a loved one. But there's little traffic, as you say. So it shouldn't be long. You have an appointment?'

Faith stared straight ahead, not daring to look behind her, even though she knew the hearse was empty. Neither did she look at her mother or Mr Samaroo. The hearse smelt of crushed Eucharist lilies and there were bits of asparagus fern sprinkled on the dashboard where the wreaths had been piled earlier. The perfume of the lilies made her feel sick.

Outside, along the street, people were stopping and looking back at the passing hearse and staring. Some pointed at the sight of the little girl and her mother sitting up front in the hearse of Samaroo & Sons with the well-known Mr Samaroo driving the empty hearse.

'This is very kind of you, Mr Samaroo. Whose funeral have you been at?' Mrs Wainwright enquired.

Faith did not want to hear the answer. She put her hanky to her nose to block out the smell of the crushed lilies. Imagine that someone she knew should see her. Imagine Clara Mendonza with the other girls seeing her. She felt that she wanted to die. No, she didn't want to die. She didn't want her mother to die. She wanted to be out of this hearse.

As Faith sat up front of Mr Samaroo's hearse, she felt sad and angry that she had lost her friends. She felt sad and angry that Clara had spoilt everything.

Faith had returned to the linen room. 'No,' she wouldn't. She couldn't. 'Don't make me.'

Just as the hearse rounded the corner near the Carnegie Library, Faith heard an hysterical choir of girls' voices, 'Faith, Faith.'

She looked to her side to see Clara Mendonza, hearing her clearly, a soprano above the others, even through the closed window, which Mr Samaroo wound up, leaning over Faith and her mother, saying, 'Such rude children, take no notice, Miss.'

'Faith, Faith.' She had to look. Clara Mendonza was laughing and dancing, winding her waist, and Faith could hear her clearly 'Fill me up, fill me up. Empty me, empty me,' in that calypso tune. She was just as she had been in the playground with her red sweet drink which was spilling out of its bottle and staining the white bodice of her uniform. 'All you, look, Faith and her mother have front seat for their funeral.'

'Put us down on the promenade, Mr Samaroo. We're just going to Le Paradis,' Mrs Wainwright fussed.

'Oh, is to the cemetery you going?' Even Mr Samaroo felt that he was going to laugh at the coincidence.

But then, he looked at Faith in her pretty white organza with the yellow butterflies. She was a truly young girl now, no longer a child, in that party dress too tight for her. She was pressing her fingernails into her hands so hard that they bled. The drops of blood fell among the yellow butterflies on her white organza. She was dabbing at the blood with her white hanky and then stuffing it into her lap, holding her stomach in pain with her clenched hand. In her mind she was speaking to Clara Mendonza. 'No, Clara, no, I don't want to see, don't make me. I don't want to do that. Look at what you've done. I'm bleeding.'

She refused to move. Her mother had to lift her down from the hearse. 'Come now, sweetheart, we'll wash it all clean.'

Faith tugged at the weeds beneath the statue of the angel with the broken arm above her grandmother's grave. She knelt in her party frock. She used to call it her twizzle dress, the one with the stick out crinolines. It did not matter anymore. It was soiled. It was spoilt. Now, where she knelt on the rough pebbles and dirt, there were brown marks.

Her mother was digging a hole, planting the gold zinnias.

Faith did not know why, but, as she knelt in the dirt with her hands smudged and her dress soiled, she began to feel better while tidying her grandmother's grave with her mother and planting the zinnias. Even her sore fingers and the blood on her best dress did not bother her anymore. Her mother looked up from her planting. They smiled at each other; understanding more than they had done for some time.

'We'll get you a new dress that really fits you. That's what you need, sweetheart,' Mrs Wainwright said to her daughter, smiling.

That Touch of Blue

About suffering they were never wrong,
The Old Masters: how well, they understood…
how every thing turns away…
Musée des Beaux Arts, W.H. Auden

She's gone. She won't ever come back.

It was on a morning, just before Christmas, when everything felt exposed because of the leafless trees. Black lines were etched against the blue and green; sky and field. The hedgerows were threadbare, but jittery with the chirp and wiggle of small birds. There was a choir of calls. There was a tinkle of running water, like many tiny bells in an underground stream. Small life, I thought.

Further away, a copse was a jagged outcrop. A row of trees was a line of camels climbing a hill. Then higher up, on Mitchel's Fold, there was a cairn. Once, on a long walk, stopping there, I had added a stone to the mound for her. I was far from home and that cairn was far from her grave in Lapeyrouse cemetery behind the blue stone wall between Ariapita Avenue and Tragarete Road in Port of Spain where the sun would be beating down and the palms would be caught by the breeze off the sea in the gulf.

I got into my car and drove down the gravel drive between the stripped beeches. I know this place in May, full and lush, breathless with chlorophyll. Snow would have been hawthorn then. Not now. I took the narrow ribbon of wet pitch into the village, turning onto the lane over the reverberating cattle grid.

*Salve Regina, Mater Misericordiae…*The monks from a Spanish Benedictine monastery near Barcelona, I think, were chanting their Gregorian music; the Marian hymn, on my cassette. I'd left it on the player from the drive up from London to Shropshire the day before. I knew it well. It took me back to those youthful aspirations, when I had left the island for a monastery in the Cotswolds. I joined in with the chant, hummed the phrase, *Vita dulcedo et spes nostra, salve!* Hail, sweet life and hope!

Indeed, there it was above me, a clear blue dome, fully emerged from the veil of mist, the rising sun shattering the windscreen, blinding me on the road to Aston-on-Clun. It could have been a sunrise in Mayaro.

You could say I was disposed to some kind of advent, some kind of coming. But the rising sun, the wet grass, the broken ice, the melting frost, the chirp and wiggle in the high hedgerows either side of the narrow lane, signalled more an Easter, a resurrection.

This was Advent time of tinselled Christingle, some newfangled, old, revived, pre-Christmas festival in the village church that I had seen the women of the parish preparing for yesterday afternoon. The last of autumn's russet bounty had been dragged in and evergreens were strewn on the floor, stuffed into crevices of stone, burgeoning from huge urns in the sanctuary under the communion rails.

We had arrived yesterday afternoon and there was still light and time enough to take our usual first walk into the village, up to the small church and make our round of the cemetery, thick with its dead and names, near the edge of the meadow.

A place to be buried or scattered.

The copper beeches clattered in the cold wind.

And, then, I saw her. She was emptying an urn of water and refilling it from a tap near the church door, swilling it out. Then she disappeared, one of the parish flower arrangers.

I thought nothing of it, then.

All was as it is at this time of the year, as I drove down to the village. *Hodie…Puer natus est.* Today…a child is born. That was not the next number on the cassette, but it could have been. It was one of the tracks, the Introit for the Christmas morning mass. I still loved the mood the chant could create, first learnt as a boy in my mountain-top school on the island, taken to early morning mass and hearing the antiphonal exchanges of the monks in choir at their Matins. It was a romanticism that has never left me. I pulled into the carpark outside the garage to buy stamps for my Christmas cards in the all-purpose village shop. This, too, was all part of this usual life that went on, regardless.

Brueghel saw it. Auden understood: how everything turns away, be it from Icarus falling from the sky or a Virgin birth.

I am no believer, but the old myths can still settle upon the landscape and open the mind to reflection on the mystery of life.

Back in my car, I pulled off the main road to Clun near the Arbor tree and climbed the small hill towards Hopesay. Say hope, we always joked, and what do you get? Hopesay. Our retreat from the world.

Just as I descended the slope from the top of the hill and rounded the bend onto the last stretch before my turn off, I slowed down because I remembered, that earlier I had noticed that the road was flooded in a dip there, so that you had to drive slowly, crossing a ford.

There was an elderly lady just ahead of me, teetering on the bank under the hedgerow, trying to cross the flooded road. I stopped, waiting so that I would not spray her. She was hesitant. I signalled for her to go ahead. But then, quite suddenly, there she was, in the car, sitting beside me.

We took the flood slowly, the water running like a stream out of the hedgerow. She was going to the church in Hopesay for the morning service, she said. I did not say anything, but I had noticed yesterday that the service was nearer to eleven o'clock that morning. She was a couple of hours too early. But I was not certain. She could have had parish duties. What business was it of mine, anyway?

She chatted on about her sons, just as my mother would in a quite different world, one of whom, she said, was coming across from Birmingham for Christmas, bringing the grandchildren. He had a good job, a manager. From time to time I looked at her. She was staring ahead and chatting away. I made encouraging sounds and assenting with 'Yes, yes.' She asked if I was from Wales? It was the old question, the lilt in my voice. I smiled and explained. She commented comparatively, on the weather between here in Shropshire and what it must be like in Trinidad.

I said I was turning off before the village, at Hesterworth, but I would take her all the way to the church. She was most obliged. I noticed that she wore a blue scarf. It was just a touch of blue fluff around her neck, sprouting under her chin from inside her buttoned up coat. It went well with her soft grey hair. She sort of sparkled.

I turned in the wide gravelled area outside the old vicarage before stopping to let her out. She thanked me, smiled. I leant over and pulled in the door. As I drove off, I noticed her in the rear view mirror, going along to the gate behind the vicarage which brought you under the yew trees to the church yard and the cemetery. That was it! Yesterday afternoon, she had been at the tap by the church door, emptying an urn of water, filling it and swilling it out.

I drove on. Then, suddenly, I was all tingly. That's how it felt. Goose pimples. Shivers down my spine. Tears filled my eyes, streamed down my cheeks. It was my mother. I had been talking to my mother. She had waited at the flood and entered the car. Then it all fell into place: the way she talked, her animated description of her children and grandchildren, pride in her son's job. I was certain. I was profoundly affected. How could this be possible? But it was.

I could not wait to get back to the flat to tell Kate.

I told her this story. Not quite like this, but the substance, the transubstantiating part of it. Her usual scepticism was confounded as she entered into the excitement of this, my unusual, Advent apparition. We had a wild idea to go looking for the lady in the church. But, by then, our usual good sense prevailed. We worked out that I had been disposed to this sensation by the mood of the Gregorian chant, the special nature of the light. Winter brilliance. That touch of blue.

The following year, at Easter, in the Green Mountains area of Vermont, as the light was fast declining on a blue day and a heavy snow was forecast, a black dog attached itself to us on our walk. It would not leave us alone. It followed us to our inn and sat by the reception door. It followed us to our chalet and sat by that door. And, again, the realisation, all tingly: my mother. She keeps appearing. There it was. I had thought she had gone forever and would never come back.

Then it peeped out, a blue name-tag on the dog's collar. That touch of blue, my mother's favourite colour.

Brueghel saw it. Auden understood, like the great masters, how we turn away.

Then, the snow came down.

A 1930s Tale:
Coco's last Christmas

This is my last Christmas in barrack yard up Pepper Hill. Even Mama say, 'Like is your last Christmas, darling, sweetheart?' Those words. Just so. What she feel? I have a feeling in my blood. I have that feeling sitting down right here, night before Christmas Eve in the dark by the window, leaning on the sill of the Demerara window, waiting for Mama. A sweet breeze only rustling the leaves in the sapodilla tree outside, coming over the cocoa hills from Montserrat, cooling down the day. But, is a lonely breeze too. And the river in the gully under the bamboo gurgling over the rocks.

Barrack yard tinkling. Barrack yard tinkling with Christmas-time music. Right down by Chen Chiney shop I hear it. The parang band practising. Bottle and spoon, tamboo bamboo, cuatro strumming: *Maria Maria Maria, Maria Magdalena* under the rum shop where Spanish and the big fellars playing cards, All Fours. And the old men, like Arnaldo Barradas, slapping down dominoes on the counter as they drink Chen rum. Whadap! Like I hear a domino fly down. I hear Spanish, 'Emelda boy!' when I come in the door. Spanish only calling me, 'Emelda boy!' Like Spanish like my Mama. Calling my Mama name so, in the shop. Running his fingers through my hair.

Mama working in big house late late.

I go miss everything here in the barrack yard. My eye brim up full full. I leaning my head on my arm. I drop off. Then my eye open big and the immense sky above me as I lean out over the window sill and look up - all the constellations of the heaven, as Father Angel would say. I learning big vocabulary from Father Angel for Exhibition class. Con stel la tions. Father Angel say the syllabic way is the best way to spell. I learning a little Latin too, and I know that *stella* is star and Mary the Virgin *Stella Maris*, star of the sea, like in the hymn we does sing after Benediction by La Divana Pastora statue. I is Father Angel favourite acolyte boy.

'You is his favourite, Theo,' Mrs Goveia, Father Angel's housekeeper say. 'Come take a little sorrel drink. Come, nice red sorrel. Take a little ginger beer mix in. I grow the sorrel myself, you know. Come, nice Christmas drink.'

She calls me Theo. Theophilus, Lover of God. I like that. Coco is another name. Coco Coco Cocorito, like the cry of a bird. Mister's name for me. I don't want to think about Mister. I have a name that does frighten me. Mister name, and it catch on. It sound like a name with softness in it.

But there is more in a name than reach the ear.

Where was I? Dreaming. Dreaming of Chantal. Chantal!

Big house like a giant Chiney lantern hanging in the sky. White and shimmering, like it make of lace. Mama late late. Chantal in there. Sometimes I think I can see her. Chantal. Chantal. I almost shouting loud loud. But is a whisper in truth. Chantal, Chantal, because I don't want neighbour to hear. I don't want neighbour to hear my business. I don't want Popo and Jai teasing me and talking talking. 'What you like that girl for? What you like that girl for? You don't see is big people. Big white people! Whitey cockroach.' Popo get vex too much. Like the big men in the rum shop.

Mama say is the times we living in. Father Angel say is living history. Men must fight for equal justice. I read it on the

Gazette I stick up on the wall. Policeman burn in Fyzabad. Spanish say one day they go burn down big house. Indian in the sugar. Black people in the oilfields.

I listen to all that. But that is not how I see Chantal.

Sometimes I sure I see her by the balustrade of the verandah, hanging over, and her long blond hair like Rapunzel in my *Royal Reader* that I have in my orange box in the corner. That is where I does learn vocabulary. Sit down in the corner on a little box stool and rest on orange box turn up. Keep my old *Red Primers* and my brown *Royal Readers* in the box by my feet crunch up. The kerosene lamp burning burning till Mama come down from big house and catch me up, wrap me against her warm skin and take me into her cosy bed. Mama.

Chantal. Sometimes I think of her spinning spinning. Mama say they have a Singer sewing machine and Chantal does sew in the bedroom.

When I go up to big house with Mama I don't go inside. I does stop by the kitchen door and peep in through the pantry door into the dining room and into the drawing room and the other room deep inside where Chantal is.

That is when Chantal don't come out and play.

Chantal must be making things for Christmas.

I hear somebody in the yard.

And down the road they still singing: 'Drink a rum and a puncha creama, drink a rum for a Christmas morning.'

Somebody in the yard. Somebody outside the window.

Voices under the window.

Not exactly voices. Sounds. Wet sounds. Like how crapeaux does sound on the wet rocks by river pool. Sschupp! Sschupp! I bend down under the window sill. Then I poke my head up little little. I peep through the crack of jalousies. Moonlight milky in the yard. I wonder that nobody didn't see me. It so bright. Moonlight flooding. Mama and my little dolly house. Like a vision, Father Angel would say. Somewhere for the Virgin Mary, La Divina Pastora to appear in all her splendour. Jewels and lace and golden crown.

I can see all Ma Procop flower garden opposite. Red red poinsettia, red turning into black in the Christmas Eve night. Because I see on the clock on Mama cabinet that it late. Is now early early morning. Christmas Eve. What I doing up so late? And Mama not home. Big house light turn off, only one light above the steps to the verandah. I imagine Chantal in her bed, in her linen sheets. Under the mosquito net making shadows on shadows. Moonlight, and Chantal golden hair falling over the side of the bed and falling down on the ground. Spinning spinning.

Maria Maria Maria, Maria Magdalena. I hearing the tune in my head.

Sschupp. Oh God, is Mama. I know my Mama even if I see her out in the night when she should be in bed hugging me up and resting her tired body. And she head not covered. She go get fresh cold. Her arms bare. Oh Mama! I know this thing. But not out in the night, not out in the moonlight for the whole yard to see, for all the parang singers coming home late to maco and abuse my Mama. Because I know that is what in Spanish voice in the shop. 'Emelda boy, Emelda boy.' Looking at me and rubbing my head and saying, 'Sugar head, sugar head.' Yes I know, I know it a long time. Long time I looking in the mirror and seeing more than Mama in my face.

My Mama black like glossy coral, her eyes like tamarind seeds. Mine green green like glass bottle at the bottom of the river. My skin like mahogany. More like Spanish skin. Cocoa 'pagnol. And me, when I look in the mirror, a real sugar head.

Brown sugar. That is why Spanish like to rub my head.

What else I see in that mirror with questions to ask my Mama? Is only me and Mama living in this house. Was so from beginning.

And he, Mister, kissing my Mama out in the yard, under the window, out in the moonlight. And more! I see his hands under her dress, playing with her silky petticoat, down inside her bosom. And those words I know on her lips, darling, sweetheart. They pass them between them like sweets they sucking. Sschupp. Mama. My Mama.

Yes, I hear Father Angel tell Mama, 'Emelda, you too pretty for your own good, child.'

Mister look up from his kisses, and I don't know whether is the moonlight or just his instinct, but I hear him in the moonlight - Coco Coco Cocorito, like he whispering in her ear, like a lizard in her ear. Looking over his shoulder at me. Like a bird on a branch at the window talking to me.

I crawl on my hand and knees like I don't hear. I crawl into Mama bed. I keep my eyes close and smell my Mama. Mama smell of vanilla and sweat. That other smell is eau de Cologne. He does put it on his face.

I don't hear her. I don't think I hear her closing the door soft soft and blowing him a kiss on the night breeze. I dream that.

The day breaking into the bedroom, yellow like allamanda trumpet flowers trumpeting from the galvanise fence. Breaking into a riot with coreilli vines with their orange pods. Sweet red seeds to suck. Iron buckets banging by the standpipes, old kerosene tin buckling, and I can hear the women and the children from down the yard.

Man done gone into the cocoa.

I oversleep. Mama gone to work in big house. The bed next

to me in her shape. The pillow is the shape of her head.

Like had a dream. Like I dream Mister come and stand under the window last night. I can hardly say it to myself in the yellow sunlight. Kiss my Mama, put his hand under her dress, caress down in her bosom. Was a dream?

Was no dream.

Maria Maria Maria, Maria Magdalena.

I busy Christmas Eve. At first is cleaning. I have to scrub the floor. I late already and hot sun have to dry it. Then I have to varnish the floor so it have time for the stickiness to vanish. I see my face in it as I shining it. Shiny and new for Christmas. Mama coming from big house with new curtains, old ones Mistress throw out. She fix them up, wash and iron. Rub down the furnitures, the Morris chairs and the little table in the centre for the vase with the new paper flowers. Touch up here and there. I is Mama factotum. Father Angel vocabulary. Mama goodboy. Mama darling.

Still I learning my vocabulary.

Then is decorations. Mama bring a set of newspaper from big house. I have to peel the old one off the wall and paste up new one. I paste and read and learn words. I already choose out the right pictures and the appropriate pictures for the different walls. I have a real nice Christmas scene in the drawing room. Is a scene from away. Is a snow scene, a real Christmas scene. Chantal say snow is what you have at Christmas. But I never see snow. We don't have snow. I know that from geography. I just know that. How snow could be the real thing? But all the picture in the paper is snow. Somebody else idea of Christmas. And all the old Christmas card Mama bring from big house from last year is snow. It pretty you know. Chantal say she making snow with Lux soap and fluff it up and let it dry. Put it on her Christmas tree. She have a real Christmas tree from Canada. I not going to bother with snow I have too much to do.

I have to cut a tree though. A nice casaurina branch. That go look like Christmas tree. And with the shiny milk-bottle top - Mama collect up a paper bag full from big house - I make decorations. Mama say I clever.

Mama leave all the preparations on the table. Pastel wrap up in banana leaf to boil. Nice ground corn and mincemeat. Every day when I pass through the kitchen, I used to give the big bowl a stir. Now bake cake. I daren't touch it. Mama Christmas cake. Heavy cake. Mama pride tell her she have to bake. Mama lucky. Luckier than many women in this yard. 'Where I go get that Emelda?' Ma Procop tell her. 'You working big house, child.' Mistress give her some of the raisins and black currants and orange peel that soaking since January. Mama keep it under the bed. By the time Advent come the room smelling like a distillery. Every now and then Mama add rum she bring from big house. She say that good to offer when neighbour and parang singers come. I sit and stir.

Then I have to run down by Chen shop to get ice. Tote ice in crocus bag, try and keep it so it don't melt. Ice to pack down in Mama ice-cream freezer. I have to stir the cream with the vanilla essence which I have to reach down from the top shelf. Mama hide it up there. I stretch and reach.

I not forget. I busy busy. But I ent forget Mister under the window.

And I still reciting vocabulary.

What for? I ask myself.

Everything ready! Mama come down five o'clock.

Mama have a story write on her face. Sometimes when she sleeping I read her face. I run my finger along her cheekbone. I read Mama story. Mama story not easy. A long story, full of pain.

'Come boy, pack ice.' Mama pour the creamy vanilla milk from the jug into the ice-cream pail. Smooth smooth it flow and twirl. Mama sprinkle grated coconut milk. She wipe the lid and screw it down and connect up the handle. 'Come, salt. Sprinkle on the ice.' Mama busy busy. She brisk. My Mama. This is Christmas. Mama come down. I know she have to go back up to big house to cook and fix Christmas for them. She come down. 'Hmm! I have to take a rest. Come boy. Darling turn this handle. Give it ten turn. Soon I go inspect it. Mistress give me a nice piece of ham bone. Look it there, put it in the kitchen when you finish turn. When Spanish and them come up we go have a real big fete tonight.'

The big hole in my heart get fill up.

Everyone in the yard on the verandah step cram up in the little house and the parang singers going sweet sweet and people dancing, stamping the floor.

Then I hear Popo say, licking ice cream from a cone, 'Theo, Theo. Watch!' When I look out the window is Chantal. Chantal in the yard. I catch her eye and she wave.

'Coco.' I hear the name she always calling me. 'Coco.' Mister name for me. What Chantal know? 'Coco.'

I go down in the yard. Then I have the hole in my heart. 'Coco.' Like I does forget to be happy when she call me that name. Theo, Theo is my name. I say to myself.

'Chantal.'

'Coco.'

'Look,' she raise her hand. 'Is for you. I make it for you. I sew it. For Christmas.'

All the time her hair in the breeze spin out like gold threads. 'Is for you. A dolly that look like you. Brown like you, like Papa's cocoa chocolate. And the green eyes, see the buttons. Is you Coco.' She laugh.

I grab the doll and run inside. I look at it and wrench the head off it and throw it in the corner of the room.

When I look out the window I see Chantal going up the hill to big house.

'Wait, wait.' I shout to her. 'Chantal.' I reach down under the bed.

'Move, all you move. Don't touch. Don't touch. Chantal!' I stand with the big windmill in my hand. It make with silver milk-bottle top, and stick on copy-book paper and papier-mâché newspaper. It paint up with red, orange and green. 'For you.'

She hold the windmill by the bamboo handle and blow on it and it spin and spin and spin.

'Feel the breeze on your face? Like sweet Christmas breeze.'

I think of the Coco doll with its head pull off.

'You going away. Papa say you going away.' Chantal blow on the windmill.

'Yes. I going town. Messenger boy. Father Angel say he don't think I could make Exhibition class again. But he say the big words will come in handy.'

'Coco.'

'Chantal, is Theo. My name is Theo. Call me Theo.' I see in her face something I see in the mirror.

The serenaders come out and fill the air, 'Drink a rum and a puncha creama, drink a rum for a Christmas morning,' going up to the La Divina Pastora church for the midnight mass.

'Theo.'
'Chantal.'
I wave. She wave.
Maria Maria Maria, Maria Magdalena.

Incident on Rosary Street

Veronica walked out onto her verandah at dawn. Rosary Street was still asleep. 'What kind of thing is this?' Three corbeaux had settled on the top branches of the mango tree in front of Miss Elcock's parlour. She pulled down Lindy's school clothes from drying on a string line. 'What all you want? Is something dead you see?'

The three corbeaux stared implacably. Judges in a court.

The hot sun had come up over the Morvant Hills and Rosary Street had shaken itself into the crash of traffic coming down the hill to the Charlotte Street junction. The galvanise roofs burned. The mango tree was too green. The sky too blue. The bright morning stung Veronica's eyes. Junior next door was singing, playing like he was David Rudder, 'Oh, Laventille, here we come. Laventille, here we come. We singing praises to your son. Oh, Laventille, here we come...'

Junior liked his music loud loud.

'King David soca sweet, oui. Even when it sad.' The boy didn't even hear Veronica.

Life on Rosary Street seemed bright for now. Too bright.

The three vultures lifted off. Their broad, black wings flapped awkwardly to lift their gawky legs off the branches: like birds now, not like judges in the court masquerading with wigs. They had scented something dead. They settled on the roof of Hing Wing's shop at the corner.

'Lindy, girl, is time to get up, oui.'

Home at No 6 Rosary Street was Veronica and her seven-year-old daughter, Lindy.

'Ma?'

'Hustle, girl. You have to go by Hing Wing for bread and milk.'

Lindy's tiny, wiry body was swallowed up in her mother's old tear-up Soca Warriors red T-shirt; her country's aspiration these many years later looked ragged now on her small child, hanging off her shoulders, unready for the barefoot walk down the hill. 'Ma, you ent give me no money, you know.'

'You go have to ask Hing Wing for trust till month end.'

'Again, Ma?'

'Unless you want to go to school with you belly empty.'

'When Daddy coming?'

'Child, what you asking me? You hear what I say. Don't talk to any of them fellas on the block.'

Lindy looked back at her mother as she descended the rickety steps from the verandah to the rough concrete path to the pavement.

'Watch the traffic.'

Veronica lost her mind in ironing Lindy's school uniform while Junior's rap base-drum beat beat against the walls next door. 'Where that child? So long she gone. I tell her don't talk to any of them stand-up-on-the-corner-sucking-their-teeth-no-where-to-get-a-work. You does talk, but do she listen to she mother? I tell you.'

Lindy had been gone far too long, long enough for Rosary Street to get that quiet feeling after the rush hour, and the pace of things to slow down before Miss Elcock opening up the shutters of her parlour at the corner of Chinnet Lane.

'You see Lindy?' Veronica called across the street to the old woman who gave her daughter sweeties to take to school.

'She ent pass yet.'

'Pass? I send she Hing Wing long time. She ent come back yet.'

Lunch time: Veronica went by the police station in Besson Street.

'Seven years old and she working the street already?' A young police officer, looking like he had just left school, joked with his sergeant at the desk.

'Officer, is my daughter you talking 'bout. My little child, my little girl,' Veronica said almost in a whisper through her teeth, she was so angry.

'You should've think of that before you send she out. What you send she out for? Where you send she? I ask you what you send she out for?'

'Food.'

'Crack! Or, some nasty man to take she in the back…'

'Man, haul your arse.'

'Madam.'

'Don't madam me till you know how to speak to people. You hear what I telling you.'

By the time the police took the complaint of the little missing girl seriously and set up their mobile unit on Rosary Street, the residents had built a bonfire of all their garbage in the middle of the street.

When a woman came running out from a back yard bawling, the street turned towards Veronica.

The woman called out for her. 'Yes, is your little girl, is Lindy.'

'Is shoot, they shoot she?' Veronica asked, her voice breaking, knowing the truth, before she was even told.

'With his bare hands he strangle she, and drop she in the hole by the cesspit,' the neighbour confirmed.

'Who do this thing?' Veronica's voice was a wail.

The fires burned all night on Rosary Street, black smoke from the pyre of burning tyres and the day's garbage.

The next morning, the corbeaux clambered back onto the mango tree to judge what was going on.

Leaving by Plane
Swimming back Underwater

The afternoon was hot.

I had set my heart upon this journey so far back that there was no turning away now. The very first enthusiasm had faded into a kind of fate. This was what was to happen. There was no changing it. I kept the growing doubt beating in my heart and fluttering in my stomach, hidden from those, whom, if they themselves had any doubts, did not show them, but only encouraged and aided me in my choice to leave, as the gospels put it, mother and father, brother and sister and country, and go follow Him.

I was giving my life to God.

I was leaving by plane that afternoon for England.

The previous weeks had been a round of farewells to family and friends, and with each event, my fate was clearer and I could do nothing about it. I was toasted and feted as if fatted for the sacrifice, my mother's Benjamin, but now Abraham's Isaac.

Would an angel descend from heaven to stay his hand?

I choked at the sight of my packed, open suitcase on the bed. There was not much to take. I would be given everything I needed when I entered the monastery. If you have a bag in the house do not go back to get it, the gospel tells us. There were a couple of shirts and most particularly long woollens, my mother's obsession with the cold I would have to suffer.

It was winter in England. It was 1963. I was just nineteen.

It was a hot afternoon. I wore a warm suit. We waited in the departure lounge for the flight to be announced. I was carrying a large bouquet of pink anthurium lilies, my aunt's gift to her sister in London. Their large fleshy hearts and erect yellow stamens pressed against the cellophane which was to save their tropical beauty from the hazards of the journey and death of the cold to come. Under my other arm I carried a shiny black Bible, the Old and New Testaments in the Douai version, a gift from another uncle and aunt.

The flight was announced and I held myself against every inclination to do the opposite thing, to run away. After kisses and hugs, I walked away without turning round till I got to the top of the steps into the plane. Then I turned and waved, like a film star.

I watched the island become a flat distance: the mountains, the plains, the archipelago between Trinidad and Venezuela.

All that I loved disappeared.

It feels now like swimming back underwater to discover what had first set me on this journey.

My first vision was when I was six and a half years old. This was a vision of the wings of the Archangel Gabriel in the church of Mary Magdalen. They turned out to be the shadow of the canopy high above the altar, an optical illusion misunderstood by a small child. Faith then was young and innocent and could deal with disappointment. The desire for visions was not dashed. Faith was learnt in the little blue penny catechism.

The school bus of white children put me down at the gate of the little red-brick Catholic church in Sainte Madeleine for catechism classes with Miss Vivy and her class of black village children and her green parrot. And so it was that we learnt our penny catechism by heart and by parrot under the sapodilla tree.

'Who made you?' Miss Vivy asks.

'Who made you?' The green parrot by the sapodilla tree repeats.

'God made me.' The first communion class answers. 'God made me.' The green parrot by the sapodilla tree repeats. 'Why did God make you?' Miss Vivy asks. 'Why did God make you?' The green parrot by the sapodilla tree repeats.

And so, on and on, at the age of seven, the age of reason, my vocabulary and metaphysical reflection expanded beyond all recognition as I learnt the theory of transubstantiation, infallibility, the immortality of the soul and what I should take most care of, my body or my soul. My soul, somewhere inside of me, was hidden, and I always imagined it was in the middle of my chest and the same shape as my heart. It was stained but capable of being made clean by confession as I embarked on a long list of sins over my first seven years. Mostly these were venial sins. The mortal ones were to come later and terrify me almost unto death and the brink of hell. These venial ones did not terrorise me, though if the truth was the truth, they added to the horrific pain of that man on the cross. I was responsible for his pain. At seven!

When I was eleven, I was ready to make my confirmation, which was earlier than usual because I was so keen. I remember my new shoes which gave me blisters, and wanting to walk up the aisle with the Lebanese girl from the convent school. There were many forbiddens there; the fact that she was Lebanese, Syrian, and also because she was a girl. I was already destined for the priesthood. That desire for the Elias girl foundered like my love written in messages at the back of holy pictures and delivered by a go-between to a Portuguese girl whom I later discovered never got my messages: my go-between, herself disappointed by her own unrequited love, pretended the cards were sent to her by her love-throb and scratched off my name and the girl's name to whom they had been sent, and inserted her own from her dearest fantasy. I discovered this flicking through her school books and finding my card. I kept silent about it, deeply shocked, angry, disappoisted that my wooing had never really occurred, but even then, saddened, and learning something about the nature of love.

Then, one night, my second vision appeared. I woke with a start, lying on the bottom bunk in the bedroom I shared with my older brother. Though now I think of it, reconstruct that memory, the bunk had been moved out and the twin beds put in, and it was the August holidays when my obsession with death and my dying was at its height. I had by the trickery of my fear won my first prize, my mother's love, taken away from my father. It was there on that bed, she by now snoring, that I awoke to Our Lady of Perpetual Help transfigured in a halo of bright light against the creamy wall of my bedroom. And as I raised myself up in bed to focus, she vanished in a flash streaking down the long corridor to my parents' bedroom where my father was asleep on his own. Our Lady was exactly as she was in the parish church of Notre Dame de Bon Secours where I had learnt to make my visits to the Blessed Sacrament since the age of seven.

At twelve I went to a boys' Benedictine boarding school in the mountains which was quite a different world from a sugarcane estate, barrack rooms, board house villages, visions and my mother's love. This was a man's world. By a strange alchemy it seemed, desire found another shape in what had been the playful antics of small boys discovering the meaning of their bodies. That rub totee time, re-formed itself with a rush of crushes on older boys. But the instruction was no affection for boys, and then there were no girls for a boarder after the stolen first French kiss during vacation, during *Love Me Tender* on the back row of the Globe cinema, the touch of a warm breast, that nest of hair, and even afterwards that clumsy attempt to enter that forbidden and secret place, that wet flower.

I chose instead a world of angels and visions. My inherited, or learned piety, continued, and I learned to serve mass, and from that very first morning when I heard the Gregorian chant of the monks in the choir, my resolve was to be one of them. This led me to leave the school and seek admission to the junior seminary where I had a good friend.

I became a builder of shrines, grottos in the mountains, imitating Lourdes and Fatima and my intense wish was that if I knelt long enough at these shrines alone in the forest, another vision would come, something more lasting, which would become more public and I would be like Bernadette of Lourdes, or one of the children of Fatima with a message for the Pope on the conversion of Russia and the end of communism in China. In these wild places, my aspirations went beyond the ordinary, and I sought to emulate the mystics, the true ascetics, with flagellations, though we often laughed that the monks whipped their pillows rather than their backs, the sound resounding through the corridors on Friday nights.

The monks in their abbey were never far from my thoughts and fantasies of my future. In their dark library I sought out books on monasticism and came upon those huge picture books from away. My favourite pictures were the portraits of monks at prayer, at work, walking in the country, standing by a lake in contemplative mood. The focus was on the tonsured head, the hands at the pottery wheel, the profile of a face enlivened by the light and shadow of candle light, the folds of the cowl, the sweep of the scapular, the silence of their hoods, their sandalled feet.

I was now resolved to be a monk, but an adolescent's chastity was a hot fever. I knelt at my bedside altar with a relic, a piece of a young Italian girl's flesh, a martyr for purity, an adolescent like myself, Maria Goretti. I kissed that dead flesh to protect my own, to enable me to say farewell to my flesh.

This was my carnival.

I woke before the servants came up. A moon hung in the window. This was my waking for the early morning mass in San Fernando when I was seventeen. I am a seminarian on vacation and must not let my term-time horarium slide.

I woke even before my parents, before my father's effervescence of Andrews Liver Salts, his daily purge, tinkles with a silver spoon in a glass as he returned down the cream corridor to his room, and my mother's cups of hot tea for him and her on a tray on her dressing table. I woke even before the night watchman leaves his post, the green bench beneath the pantry window, where he sleeps and pretends to watch over us against the thief from the barrack rooms and board house villages along the road into San Fernando, now enslaved to my memory. I hear the voices from the barrack rooms. I hear the screams. 'He chop she. He chop she.' I feared that desperate chopping, their frightening poverty, bush rum, love and tabanca, the passion of their unrequited loves which delivered them to death. I feared what I might see hanging upon the branches of a mango tree on Hang-Man Alley.

Our trust is in God and the black man, our watchman, against the treachery of the coolie. That is what I overheard on the verandah.

The house is untouched from the night before, the house with the Sacred Heart enthroned, and last year's Palm Sunday palms twisted and dried, stuck behind the frame, scraping against the cream concrete.

It is still dark for me to see the beam from the headlights of the Princes Town bus coming up over the cusp of the hill like a pantomime moon directed by an erratic child. The racatang box of a bus freewheeled into the sugarcane gully after its grinding climb up from Monkey Town. It sounded already exhausted with its journey from Barackpore, but it still had to climb the hill from Wellington. When it starts its climb in the bend where the Roman Catholic chapel used to be in a barrack room, it changes down into first gear for the steep climb past the Canadian mission school.

When I hear this sound, this is the sign to kiss my mother's cheek and say I am gone, leaving my father to understand my leaving. 'Your father is not a demonstrative person,' she says. It meant that I yearned for his love and could not feel it. It was an exercise in absolute faith, a belief in the invisible, and when it was given I was so enraptured that I could not hold it. It shattered like a crystal glass falling on the pantry floor: dramatic, incandescent, dangerous. I went into the dawn without his touch.

I kept my mother's kiss between the pages of my gold-edged missal, marked with an image of Dominic Savio, another teenage saint of purity to counter the gyrating pelvis of Elvis Presley *Shaking All Over*, at the Rivoli theatre. My lips had opened at the confessional grid with words I had even once told my mother of the fever of my sin, which was then made pure for communion with a decade of the rosary. My kiss on her cheek came with me out into the yard and down the gravel gap past the whispering casaurinas and the moonlight shadows of the tamarind tree, till I came to stand by the pitch road near the Chiney shop for the bus driver to pick me out in his beam.

As I entered the bus with its brown wooden shutters against the dew and fresh colds, I entered another music far from the Roman Catholic hymns of the parish, or the Gregorian chant of the monks who taught me at school in the mountains of the north.

I entered the night of black skins turbaned in white cotton, still trembling with drums silenced by the dawn, made hesitant by history. Their percussion had been silenced, that music and singing which conjured Shango inside Saint John the Baptist. The gods of one place inhabit the saints of another, that is the belief of the people, if not of my mother's priests. See the circle, hear the bell, Shouter Baptists by Library Corner. 'These people are impossible,' my mother said.

This is the world which formed me to choose that journey to give my life to God. I can see that now. Though it was not the desire for the supernatural this time, but the vision of the transfigured poor.

As I travelled on to San Fernando, I recited the villages like my rosary beads: Diamond, Esperance, Palmiste, Cocorite, Union Hall where I was conceived in the overseer's house. Over the fields, Golconda by the teak trees. As I opened the shutters and looked out into the villages I heard again Daisy, my mother's servant's voice telling me her Hindu wedding stories when we went out on Sunday afternoons to see the wedding car passing in the road like a Hosay with bamboo and crepe paper and Christmas-time tinsel, housing bride and groom and page in satins and net and jewels, yellow gold from Patel's in San Fernando, car horn blaring, Hindi music screaming. 'See the little boy,' she says, 'he sleeps between them to make sure they don't jook in the night.' They astonished me, boy and girl and baby boy. I tried hard to imagine them ribboned together in bed, children in the night of the galvanised barrack room that wedding night. 'Jook she! Jook she!' I kept hearing Daisy's voice.

Then here we were at the Cross-Crossing down by the Cipero River before it reached Embarcadier. I slumbered, jostled against the warm shoulders of a market woman going into Mucurapo market with crocus bags of ground provision, a hand of green fig stored under the seat.

As the bus went in and came out of the potholes, she cradled me with my prayer books on my knee. 'You is the madam child from Picton?' I nodded, glad to be recognised and given an identity in this night of a bus.

My mother's fame had spread far into the foothills of Monkey Town and Barackpore. School children walked miles barefoot to learn catechism at my mother's knee under the cream bungalow; black children, not Indians. They went to the Canadian mission and Presbyterians to get their Christian God and education. What black children got was more - my mother, Coca-Colas, the Pope's infallibility and the transubstantiation of bread and wine into the body and blood of Christ. If they could learn the little blue penny catechism by heart, the black parish priest would let them make their First Communion, and the Irish archbishop would come all the way from Port of Spain into the country to confirm them in their faith with a slap on the cheek.

When we arrived in San Fernando, the kind black woman said, 'You grow into a fine boy, say a prayers for me.' She let herself down into Mucurapo Street letting in the light and the smell of freshly cut oranges.

The pandemonium of the early morning coming into market banged around in the bus grinding up Mucurapo to where it crosses with Lord and Coffee Streets. The cocks were crowing a new morning, echoing betrayal in my ears: a cacophony of car horn, cart wheel, newspaper boys, '*Gazette, Guardian*', and the poor Princes Town bus straining up the hill to the Library Corner.

It had been part of my adolescent asceticism to travel by the bus on the hard wooden seats rather than take a taxi from out of Diamond Village. What was my asceticism but life for others. Our lives were confused. The market woman had no other way to travel.

I came out into the hot sunshine and the blinding light to climb up from Library Corner to Harris Promenade past the Presbyterian church to the Roman Catholic church of Notre Dame de Bon Secours, Our Lady of Perpetual Help. Down the road, the other side of the town hall, was the Anglican church. These were the two thieves on either side of Christ on Calvary. That is how I was taught to see the three churches of the promenade.

The promenade is opposite to my old primary school, 'Boys School'. It is the boys' RC school, smelling of coconut oil and Indian children smart at sums. They are my pardners: Espinet, Redhead and Ramnarine. On the promenade are statues of Mahatma Gandhi and Uriah Butler, the Oilfields Workers' Trade Union's leader. There is a bandstand. Race and politics, politics is race. History is not simple and the meaning of freedom is different; bread of freedom broken is a different bread, some eat cassava, some flour.

The freedom I walked into was the freedom and theatre of

the high-vaulted church built by my uncle. I rest here, at last, arriving at church for morning mass. I genuflect, enter my pew. I kneel among the family names on brass plaques: Lange, Farfan, de Verteuil, Agostini, de Pompignon, d'Abadie. I learn that religion is privilege.

Introibo ad altare Dei.
  Ad Deum qui laetificat juventutem meum –
  Indeed, the joy of my boyhood was this. I knew no other joy except sin, the sin of impurity; that blinding delicious passion, jocking, which locked out all fear until twilight, and then out of that darkness came fear of death and hell, kept at bay with fingers chained to my rosary beads. For I also knew the excitement and pleasure in the afternoons or evenings in the palaces of Hollywood: the Empire on Penitence Hill, the Globe, Radio City, Gaiety and the New Theatre, which gave me bad thoughts to fight against, and then having to make my act of contrition. Then, sleep might come like a balm. Morning brought the hope of confession and starting all over again. It was a treadmill: purity, sin, impurity, confession.

It comes back with a rush, like swimming back underwater. The afternoon was hot. I was giving my life to God. I was leaving by plane for England. It was winter in England. I clutched my bouquet of pink anthuriums. The yellow stamens drooped, the petals folded. There were drifts of snow like on Christmas cards. Day was dark like night.
  What had I done? This was now irrevocable.

One day, at the height of that first spring, I sat alone in the middle of a field of buttercups and daisies with a notebook on my knee, and holding my Parker fountain pen, given to me by my father, passed down from my grandfather with his initials, my own initials, his, inscribed on the barrel. It was one of the few possessions I was allowed to keep which connected me to home. I was absorbed in writing my monthly letter to my parents.

Crouched there, concentrating, I had not noticed them encroaching upon me. There was a strong sense that I was not alone. There was the rustle of the leaves among the chestnuts and copper beeches. There was the fragrance of spring grass and cow parsley. I was lost in my thoughts, but there, so near, that presence.

When I turned around I saw that I was surrounded by a herd of young bulls. They stood and stared. I froze. Then I panicked. Clutching my notebook and pen I got up and started running down the field towards the gate where I had first entered earlier that afternoon. When I turned around to check on my pursuers, they had not moved. They stood, the entire herd, staring, young bulls perplexed by my antics.

As I tried to compose myself, control my fear, I realised, that in my rush to escape, I had dropped my fountain pen inscribed with my grandfather's initials. Days after, when the field was empty, I tried to find my pen, which had come to represent everything I had left behind at home. I never found it. I had lost that connection to home. The feeling overwhelmed me. It frightened me, what I had done, leaving my mother, father, home and country to find God.

The Last Glimpse of the Sun

There are those who belong to their home, and these others clinging to their exile.

Filibustering in Samsara Tom Lowenstein

She was one of these, pressing her loss to her breasts, carrying her exile in her heart. There were tears and the void that hurt. Fire and noise. That was the nature of her exile. She had lost him. She was on her own now.

She had come north. The latitude was the same as the north of Scotland. 'This is the Arctic,' joked her friend, Åsa, in her letter, which Iseult had read in her London flat. 'Wrap up,' she had advised. Spring would be later there, at the end of May, after they had collected all the dead leaves of the last autumn and the antlered branches of the long winter, casting them upon the huge bonfires at their end-of-winter parties.

Iseult was arriving for Easter in Gothenburg, or 'Göteborg', she whispered, as she remembered from previous visits sounding her G as a Y, observing her Swedish accent, letting herself daydream as the plane from Heathrow began its descent.

She could see that the snow had not yet melted in the forests. The lakes were still frozen. As the stewardess collected up the litter, Iseult reflected on the comforts she took for granted now as she drained the last of her gin and tonic. She let herself enjoy these small comforts. She let them anaesthetise her.

They were almost on the ground and she could see the frozen lakes near the airport. Skating? She had never skated on ice, or even walked on ice, at least not on these kinds of open expanses of lake ringed by forests as old as the first spring after the ice age. Ice, two metres deep.

As they taxied into their bay, she shut her eyes. She heard a voice from a previous visit. 'Like gunshot, the melting ice,' Sven had said. Then he had described it as they walked along the dirt paths made soft with pine needles. 'The cracking ice, breaking up, like gunshot, again and again. Veins would splinter and run wild, opening up fissures, chasms, beneath the surface.' Iseult wondered whether Sven would be there this time. He had spoken in a trance and she had let herself follow him. In her mind now, she stood on the brink of one of those chasms in a world unbelievably cold. There was gunshot going off again and again. So much had happened since she had last been here, had last seen Sven. None of it had anything to do with here.

Åsa was there in Arrivals and they immediately fell into each other's arms.

'Hi.'

'Hi! Welcome!'

Instantly, their close relationship, forged over years, was resumed, though they saw each other only about once a year now if they were lucky. They had kept up this friendship since university days when Iseult had first come north as an au pair one holiday. What was important now was that Åsa could also share her most recent experience of the island. She had come and stayed on the island twice when Iseult was first there. Åsa loved the light and heat of the tropics after the long dark winters.

It was not that Iseult did not value their closely shared experiences from their early past, but, now, she needed to be with people who had shared her experience of the island. Not that she always wanted to talk about it, quite the contrary, but just the fact that they had been there was what mattered. Åsa would understand when any kind of reference was made in passing. She knew the beauty of the place. She understood how important it was, what was being achieved there, and what had happened. She also knew about Peter.

'You remember Sven?' Åsa lit a candle on the windowsill. It was like night outside. 'Thought he'd cheer you up.'

'Cheer me up?'

'He'll be good for you.'

'Good for me?'

'Come on. You know. You must move on after Peter.'

Then, they giggled over their gin and tonics, like when they were young girls falling into each other's arms.

'Everything's so different now. Isn't it?' Iseult talked aloud to herself.

'Yes.' Åsa listened from the kitchen. 'But...you know. You must...'

Dinner was like it always was at Åsa's. Delightful, delicious! Crayfish! In this country of candles, the smallest meal, the simplest, even breakfast, partook of the solemnity which lighted candles give to a meal. A kind of sacramentality, she thought. They ate their sill and potatoes with hard bread.

'My mother always lit a candle on waking and took it to the breakfast table.' Åsa lit a second candle on the table.

'Warmth?

'Yes.'

'Sven's late.'

Iseult and Sven held each other in their gaze for an instant while Åsa was fixing coffee. They were both reflected in the glass of the windowpane with candles, and the table littered with the remnants of their meal. On the wall above them, embroidered in a wreath of spring flowers, the word, *Återlöst*.

'What does it mean?' Iseult asked, looking at Sven.

'Redeemed,' he answered. 'You've been working in the Third World since I last saw you, involved in politics?'

'Redeemed?'

'Yes…'

'Curious how…'

'What?'

No. She would not be drawn. She didn't want a discussion on imperialism and colonialism. She knew the signs, settling into comfortable armchair radicalism with coffee and brandy. The Third World, it sounded like some kind of other world, a planet, a galaxy, out there, spinning away in its own orbit. Where?

'It's been a while back. Åsa visited me. Didn't she tell you? Åsa, did you tell Sven…?' Iseult tried with hesitation to play down any sign of importance that might be attached to Sven's questions. Then she hoped she had not sounded too nervous.

'Yes. I'm sure I told you Sven? Last time I came back from out there.'

Out there? Falling off the edge of the world. She had a friend on the island who always teased her about that colonial expression, 'coming out to the island'. From where? She used to ask?

Åsa came back with more coffee. 'Another brandy, anyone?'

The world. The globe, when she spun it as a child, had different colours. 'It's mostly pink,' she had said to her father.

'That's because we own most of it.' Empire, such an expansive word. Then it lost its mystique because it always sounded like, umpire, to her. Now, a kind of meaningful pun, she thought. Somewhere, far away, she heard Sven's voice, 'Yes, of course, you told me about it. Yes, the island, and what had happened.'

On a previous visit, Iseult had noticed the increasing number of black immigrant children who had been adopted by white, blond parents. She wondered about their growing up. It could be fine. It could work out, she supposed, leaving the oppressiveness of the thought. She had wanted a child with Peter. Thoughts like that bruised the mind too much now; puzzling out the world, and her own life, shattered. She switched off the newsreel in her head, shut out the colour supplements with their photographic art of hunger and starvation, read while spooning through boiled eggs with toasted soldiers, toast and marmalade on blue, willow-pattern china, on Sundays which stretched yawningly and empty as she opened the papers. Her London life. She shut out the personal and the political.

'We have got an immigrant problem here now.' Sven announced the state of affairs. Or, was it the sense of deliberateness in not speaking in his own language, which leant that heavy serious tone to his talk. Iseult frowned.

'Oh yes? Tell me about it.' Iseult was eager to stay here rather than go over there.

Sven talked. She heard him without listening. So often now she found herself drifting off in the middle of conversations. Her mind was indeed shattered, all of her life, she thought.

She suddenly had this very clear picture of a cliff-side on the island above the small main town, terraced like an English seaside town, rusty galvanised roofs in the hot sun and the bay below green and blue. It had been quarried in an instant. Gunshot and mortar shells exploding. Red dirt. She remembered that it was the absence of the dark green trees that she had noticed first of all in the morning when she threw open the window after the terror of the night, huddled together with neighbours under tables and beds while the bombs fell, like they were falling in the garden and would soon fall on top of their house. There was still smoke rifling up into the blue air, like the smoke from an innocent bonfire on an autumn afternoon, she thought, in the allotments at the back of London terraces.

Sven exhaled the smoke from his cigarette and it twirled into the overhanging table lamp. Leaning back, he looked handsome in an ugly kind of way. 'You're still so brown.' he said.

'Yes, everyone keeps saying that, "You're so brown".' The sun must be an idol in a place she imagined as one of the fjords and glaciers, going further north for her myths. Forests of serene pine. Silver birches. The silence of snow.

Åsa rolled a joint.

'Nice.' Sven smiled.

This precise ritual of laying out, smoothing, sprinkling, rolling and licking, twisting and lighting took Iseult back to the sixties. That was where it had all started; the transgression of that time. She had always liked photography. The time came back as stills. Paris and Prague, 1968. Now she couldn't listen. Was it the sixties? Was it then that she had taken up the burden to change the world? What a thought! It seemed now that she had taken it up much earlier. Inhaling the hash made her drift off even more. Sven was still asking his questions. 'Was it difficult for you being white in a black country?'

It had been laid on her small shoulders as a child, burning

and bruising her skin with that first hot sun, a white child in a black country. Her father flicking the pink globe. Then she was at the bottom of the gravel drive. The verges were dry grass. Her father had fenced off their land from the rolling land. 'Africa,' he used to say, pointing into the distance. Now she was standing at the gate with him. Her father wore white and khaki. She had on a white muslin dress with small blue flowers, puffed sleeves and a sash, which was tied in a bow at the back. Her hair was in plaits and she had one leg up on the gate, climbing to reach the face of the black man her father was talking to. This was Molefe who worked on their farm. They were all smiling. That was the last photograph taken before they had to leave Avalon for England. Home for home, saying goodbye to their old family farm and her nurse, Annie. They called her that. Whenever Iseult asked why they were leaving, they said, 'Mau Mau'. It was a strange sound, 'Mau Mau'.

'Do you want some more?' Åsa passed the joint. Iseult waved it on.

She didn't really smoke anymore. She didn't need any assistance with the everlasting newsreel. She didn't want it speeded up. She regretted now that she had had even that small amount.

The newsreel continued.

A student hurls a rock stone in Soweto. The running child gunned down. A child in Vietnam runs down the street burnt by napalm. They run together with the children on the island, leaping off the red cliff under the fort. There was the story on the island of the Caribs in the seventeenth century, hurling themselves in death to the rocks below, rather than surrender to the invading French.

The scratched record played Dylan's 'We shall overcome some day...' Sven was still talking. 'We don't understand anything about the Third World. That's why we're having problems. We're insular.'

'But you have a progressive government. Neutrality in the war. Olaf Palme was a champion of the Third World, a friend of Castro's, Michael Manley, Ortega. He supported the struggles in Cuba and Nicaragua.'

'The government, yes, but not the people. The government absolves us. Bureaucratic justice leaves no room for a personal decision.'

Iseult could see what Sven meant. She had learnt that lesson herself. Discipline. Defence. The Militia. She had joined up. Peter joined up after her. At first she had to convince him to support the struggle. Then everyone was joining up preparing for the rumoured US invasion. They had become more and more isolated internationally. They stood alone, supporting the USSR's invasion of Afghanistan, the banning of Solidarity in Poland. But she also knew how much had been achieved in a short space of time: education, housing, health care, wealth distribution, justice. A big revolution in a small place, Castro had called it. You saw the world depending on where you stood, from where you looked. Her father used to flick his pink globe and watch it spin. How peaceful to have things taken care of for you. How much more difficult to act. Difficult to act, dangerous to leave it to others. It was a dream, a dream to change the world.

'Yes.' Iseult answered, buried deep in her own thoughts, losing the thread of the discussion. She realised then that Åsa had left the room, crashed out. She was alone with Sven with the candles burning down. The old record scratched away, 'The answer my friend is blowing in the wind...' She remembered Sven's blue eyes undressing her. Then she heard her own small voice far away. 'More, there, there, more…'

The loss which she felt was for Peter's kerosene-lamp-lit room in a small board house in the bush along a rutted pitch road. This was how they used to meet when they had first met, young lovers. Then it changed. After the initial persuasion, which was her persuading him, to join up, Peter became now more than ever involved. At times she felt that he just enjoyed the excitement of it all, young fellas with Kalashnikovs. Often, he was not there at home. On many nights she would lie awake waiting. She remembered the cockerel was crowing at midnight; its crow of betrayal; Peter's crow, she had come to call it. Miss Girot along the road had always kept fowls in her yard. Peter used to tap on the window when he arrived, not to startle her, she thought, by just entering unannounced. She remembered seeing his black face against the black of the night. It was burnished by the glow of his cigarette. He was all in shadow at those times, an almost invisible presence. He was so excited when he got back so late. Her one aim then was to soothe his stricken spirit with the tips of her fingers. His body was rigid, throbbing, and ready to spring like a loaded gun at the slightest rustle in the night. 'You want some food?' She asked him, wanting something normal. He would brush her aside, trusting no one or anything, as he made the room secure with his revolver and himself sure that she was the only person in the house. He was like a boy playing cops and robbers. 'After, keep the food for after.' His words were muttered, almost inaudible. Then it was the ritual borne of his excitement, his fear, she thought. He would pin her arms against the wall of the bedroom with one hand, where she had followed him in his surveillance. Like something he had seen in a Hollywood film, she thought. His other hand tore at the light T-shirt she wore in the heat to sleep. He buried his head in her breasts, finding her nipples, sucking hard, biting, chewing, until she cried and he stifled those cries with his palm, leaving her T-shirt stretched across her throat. She could hardly breathe. She wouldn't struggle. He released her arms. Then he went down, kneeling in front of her, so her hands, now freed, played with the tight curls on his head. Anything, she thought, she would do, to regain some of the love she had felt for him. He licked and kissed her belly. He buried his face between her legs in her pubic hair, his tongue finding the salty crack with the slightly fishy taste he had said that he liked. She did not move. She was made as taut as his muscles as his fingers separated her labia, to touch the tip of her clitoris. She knew that this was when she had to guard herself. This was when the silence was so intense that she could hear the sea in the bay, the salt water sucked in and meeting the fresh water of the small river, which emptied itself below the house. She could not give herself up to this or to him. She could not let herself take pleasure in this for herself. She kept guard. He kept pulling her down, so she slid her back down against the wall to meet him and let him take her mouth in his. 'Come, come and lie down,' his voice releasing an utter of tenderness. Then he changed his mind and stood her up against the wall again. She could feel his revolver pressing against her cervix. She allowed the ritual. Then the tension in his body relaxed. He went and lay on the bed on his stomach. She massaged his back and neck, his buttocks, behind his knees. He closed his eyes. She kept guard. Then, they would fuck. Again, she would try to retrieve that something they called love, though she knew she had lost him to what he called the Revo. Only after that, he ate the food she had prepared for him. But she knew she had lost her boy; he had seemed so young when they had first met, though in fact they were the same age. She had loved his youth, his island and its young revolution to which she had committed herself.

'So, you've arranged to meet Sven this weekend,' Åsa said at breakfast, lighting her candles like her mother had always done.

'Oh, yes, I'd almost forgotten. I must've fallen asleep before he left. You had already crashed out. He must've let himself out. Poor man.'

'I'm sure he was fine. He can look after himself. He called while you were still asleep. I said that you could both use the summer house if you wished.'

'But, I've come to see you.'

'My parents are up this weekend. It's Easter weekend. Good Friday, today. Besides, it would be really useful if someone went down and turned on the water, opened up the house for them. They are due to go down after Easter. Don't feel guilty. You're here for a good time. Yes? Time to move on. You used to like him long ago. We'll see each other next week for as much time as we like.'

'When's Sven coming round?'

'At three.'

Iseult climbed the hill behind the block of apartments in the Lagerbringsgatan. At the top was an outcrop of rock from where she had a view of the city. The last time she had come here she had stripped off her top and sunbathed. Today it was freezing. The sky was ice blue. The rock pools were frozen. Like mirrors in the vivid light, cold even for a Swedish Easter. She sat in a sun-catch where a screen of evergreens provided a windbreak. Today was *Lång fredag*. Long Friday, she translated. That day must've seemed very long, she thought, that day when a man carried a cross up to a small hill outside the city, to a place of execution and was crucified there. Maybe, because she was now in the north, and it was Good Friday, the Anglo-Saxon poem, *The Dream of the Rood*, which she remembered studying at university, came back to her. Long ago, she thought, celebrated in broken lines, the tree spoke of the young hero who had climbed into its branches and embraced his crucifixion. Heroes chose death, Iseult reflected. Torture destroys time. An instant can be eternal. A week can seem like yesterday. Iseult hugged herself against the cold. The terracotta roofs below, bled. Iseult thought of Peter. Where was he? Everything had happened so quickly. She heard her friend Pearl's voice. They had had to lie flat on the ground. No one knew where the shots were coming from, ricocheting among the rafters of the old colonial building. Women and children, everybody lying down, face down on the floor. This was when they heard the gunshots outside in the courtyard. Somebody shouted, 'They kill them!' It was only when she returned to London and had seen the French journalist's film of the children leaping off the side of the cliff with the big guns trained on them, running with the shots in their backs, that she understood the full extent of what had taken place. They had used the guns on their own young people. She could not believe that of Peter. She hoped that he had not been there. Where was he the night that the Prime Minister and the other ministers had been killed? Then, the Americans invaded. She was evacuated. Rescued, was what the British Airways' stewardess called it, after they had been airlifted by chopper to a neighbouring island to catch the flight back to London. Iseult remembered the immigration officer looking up at her from her passport, as he read Kenya for her birthplace. '*You* born in Africa?' He smiled a wry smile as he smiled with his question.

She remembered, that on the plane she had sat staring out at the wing, glinting. She kept on staring until the last glimpse of the sun had vanished.

Like in a dream, it seemed like that now. He was beside her, naked in the heat, then inside of her. He's emptying all his fear into me was her thought. When she looked up at his face there were beads of sweat on his brow and cheeks. Like the tribal markings on some Africans. She remembered a man with markings coming to their farm. Her father gave him food. But she could hear her Aunt Thelma's voice, 'Filthy Kaffir.' She could feel his semen trickling down her leg. Her aunt's voice was still echoing from another dream, it seemed. 'Filthy Kaffir.'

Then, Miss Girot's cock crowed. It crowed three times. He was not there to explain anything to her, if he had even known.

There were the helicopters and the bombs. Miss Girot came with Ma Rosie to hide with her in the house. In the morning, she saw the hillside with the red dirt where a bomb had fallen. At the corner was a GI with a rifle slung over his shoulder. 'Hi, you guys!' He was chewing gum.

She felt that she had lost her lover and what had become of their revolution. She would not have his child. Both had betrayed her.

Iseult looked at her watch. It was three o'clock. The young hero had climbed onto his cross. It was three o'clock. It had grown dark.

Sven turned on the water in the shed at the back of the summer house. Iseult made the beds in the room upstairs.

Near the summer house was a wooded hillside. Iseult remembered that the last time she was here, the hill was in flame. It startled her. 'It was all red and yellow,' she said to Sven who was chopping wood for the open fire. Now, in between the evergreens and the gleaming lines of the silver birches were the wintering deciduous branches.

'When you get to the top of that hill you can see a small lake on the other side,' Sven explained.

They went out before the light had completely disappeared. But when they descended the other side to the shore of the lake it was a different place to what she had remembered. It was a different place in a different season. The lake was frozen. 'Come, take my hand, but mind your step.' Sven was reassuring. Gingerly, Iseult placed her foot on the frozen lake. She'd never done this before. All around, the silent forest ringed them in. The silence rang for miles. Then, Sven's voice again: 'Like gunshot, the melting ice, the cracking ice, like the shot of a gun going off again and again as the veins splinter and run wild, opening up fissures, chasms beneath the surface.' He was telling her his winter's tale, which he had told her before. He was tender and she felt that she had to guard against that. She could not give herself again and then lose it all.

'Tell me what it was like when you were younger.' They huddled around a fire among a hearth of stones, barbecuing sausages on spiked sticks. The wood smoke was getting into their clothes and hair.

'I liked it when we slept in the forests under the stars, lying close for warmth. I was training to be a youth leader then.'

'With other boys?'

'Yes'

'Young men together. Young heroes. Yes?' Iseult got up and strode across to a huge rock, which was covered with a pelt of moss and small lichens. She could feel herself getting angry. She stroked it as she would the flanks of a large animal. She turned and leant her back against the stone with her arms stretched out in cruciform. 'A huge beast. It's like the back of a huge beast.'

'Like a beast, a wild sleeping beast.' Sven smiled. She could see that he was humouring her. Her mood changed. She walked ahead of him now, visiting the small outcrops of rock, like a pilgrim. In her grey coat she was camouflaged against the lattice of silver birches with their peeling barks. She imagined that an elk was standing there in front of her.

'Once I was picking mushrooms, and I looked up suddenly. I must've felt him. He was upon me. He reined himself away. Extraordinary! He had stumbled upon me, where I was, bent low, picking mushrooms. Then he dropped down the side of a dip in the land. He disappeared, but I could feel him still. Then, I noticed the forest move and a small herd shifted like shadows, almost imperceptibly. Antlers like branches.'

Back in the house, they sat on the floor in front of the fire.

'How did you know it was a he?' Iseult put another log on the fire. She no longer cared for the winter's tale Sven had told her in the wood.

'It must've been. I didn't think. It was…'

'Were you scared?' The flames were licking the chimney.

'Oh, yes! I thought he would attack me.'

'She, maybe. It could've been she.' She felt an anger rising in herself.

The fire roared.

The creases around Sven's lips and nose twitched and Iseult

felt glad and relieved to notice his fear and hear him admit it. She had known fear. She held his face in her hands. He was still afraid, she could tell.

'Young men together, and you were still afraid, young heroes?' She was looking into his eyes. Hers were full of questions, angry questions.

She tugged at his jumper and pulled it over his shoulders and head. Then she deliberately unbuttoned each button of his shirt down to his navel where the blond hair bristled out of his groin. Like curls of flame the hair licked up the middle of his stomach. The blond hair ran up and filled his chest and circled his nipples. She leaned over and bit them. He winced.

Sven lay on the floor, loose against the cushions from the sofa. Iseult straddled his legs. She needed this position.

She now needed each detail of his body from the roots of his hair, which she parted and ruffled. She held his head in her hands and kneaded his cheeks. 'Young men together,' she repeated. 'Heroes!' She spat into his mouth.

The fire crackled in the open hearth.

Iseult pulled off Sven's unbuttoned shirt and slipped down his belly, unbuckling his belt, opening up his trousers and quickly yanking them off with his underpants at the same time over the rump of his bottom.

She slid back from him. She knelt between his legs unlacing his shoes, pulling them off and then his socks. He lay naked before the open fire in the glowing heat.

Sven's penis was erect against his belly. Iseult leaned forward between his outstretched legs. With her face in his groin, she pulled his penis into her mouth. She sucked on it awkwardly. Then she pulled herself up and went down again with her open mouth to suck on it again. She lifted herself and straddled him, fitting his penis into her vagina. She raised herself up, not touching him with her hands, moving slowly in rotations around the length of him inside of her. She seemed to almost leave him, then descend again. All the while, she delivered her incantation with rising anger, 'Young men together! Heroes!' She spat it out.

The fire blazed. The burning logs sang. In the distance, Iseult could hear gunshot, the ice cracking again and again, and opening up chasms beneath the surface of the lake on the other side of the hill.

She lifted herself away from Sven. She could feel his semen trickling down her leg.

She knew that she needed the heat of the fire on her back. She had needed the black night and the small cottage, somewhere along a rutted road in the bush, closing in on her, on him.

Her shoulders burnt like they had when she was a little girl in the hot sun in Kenya, far away in Avalon. The island shone and shone till the last glimpse of the sun on the green of the leaves.

Then, all that she had loved, disappeared.

Prophet

This is the dark time, my love
Martin Carter

I had come back to write about a nineteenth-century painter, an ancestor of the old family, and ended up reporting on something quite different. Sasha called from London a week after I had arrived back. 'Patrice, can you do the story?' I could barely hear him through the drifts of snow I had just seen on the news.

'Which story?'

'Come on man, where are you? I know you. You're living in your head.'

'No, I'm living on the Saddle Road, Maraval.'

'What!' he screamed down the phone. I didn't even have to lower the air conditioner or the cable - strictly tennis - both of which I have at high decibels as a way of keeping the roar of traffic out of my apartment: a tropical blizzard.

'Take it easy, Sasha.'

'You know what you just said?' he screamed.

'What?'

'It's where it's happening.'

'What?' Then I lost him to the airwaves and the snow.

I emailed him. Speaking to Sasha on the phone is like being bludgeoned. This is what I told him, trying out my landscape pieces:

In the morning, I begin my walk in darkness and finish it just as the first light of dawn bleeds into the grey foreday morning. The ridges above me are the first to be lit where I walk among the villas of the rich in the valley of Maraval, an old suburb of Port of Spain. I've kept this up since my arrival. It's the one certain thing which I do at the moment. So much else is guessing. What are you telling me? P

Beautiful, beautiful! And this guy, your artist, he did watercolours? I can see it in your language. But Patrice, read the papers. Look at the news. This is something for you. I know you can write about this. I know you'll want to write about this. Sas

Funny, I thought. Why doesn't Sasha just tell me what he's talking about?

I read the papers the following day. First day I bought the papers since my arrival. By the time I leave the apartment and the nineteenth century in the afternoon they are all sold out. I would never buy a paper just before or after my walk, spoil my fraction of the dawn when I can hear myself think.

I read the articles on last year's missing children and an editorial. There were no leads on the children. I felt I was going to be sick. Then I went down to the main police station. 'Who are you? You have a press card?' I overheard the talk: they were busy dealing this morning with the case of two stray police bullets injuring two infants in Carenage last night during a shootout. Nothing to do with the children I was seeking a lead on.

This is a small island, Sas, that last year had a murder

each day. The Chief Justice is on bail and under some kind
of house arrest for alleged corruption. The leader of the
opposition in the parliament is on bail also for alleged
corruption. Everyone says, 'He tief man!' There is a
connection somewhere, they say. All of this I have just
learnt. P

Fascinating. But keep to the story. Sas

I pass the police each morning on my walk coming up to the
Chief Justice's villa behind high walls and slavering dogs. They
put their lights on bright and catch me in the full beam. They
slow down and take a good look. I can't believe it's my jogging
shorts. I get cold sweats with police, a hangover from the
sixties and seventies in a homophobic metropole.

I'm beginning to feel at home, but still missing the old,
deserted estate house at Versailles in the Montserrat hills.
Don't miss that narrow life though. I try out a next piece on
Sasha:

The clouds in the nineteenth century must have been the
same over Saut d'Eau and the lit ridges of Paramin, the
same gentle hills which welcome the seraphic flight of white
egrets, the first birds to bless the valley as I begin my walk
along Collens Road. And the nineteenth century, think
what happened then! P
PS I went to the police station - no luck.

Keep digging. Keep writing. Sas.

As Sasha had first said, I was lucky with the apartment on

Saddle Road - with the position that is. The block was built in the late fifties, early sixties, and the old fella that I bought from had changed nothing over the years. So the best which can be said about the interior decor is that it has a distinctly retro look. I won't ever change the lampshades. 'Right at the centre of things,' the agent had said. I don't think she understood her own irony.

I'm definitely doing the story. How can I not? P

Sasha would know what I meant without asking me to go there.

Opposite the school from which the children have allegedly been abducted! What a coincidence! Now I saw my luck. Somehow I can't imagine it. Not here, not from Miss Beaubrun's School. 'That won't do!' I can hear her at prayers in assembly every morning as she shrieks out the national anthem and the children scream it out after her, echoing: 'Islands of the blue Caribbean sea...where every creed and race find an equal place!' Hmm! 'God bless our nation!' Hmm!

Some of those mites, gone? Their voices fade when I shut the door to the verandah. I find myself standing in the middle of the lounge looking through the glass doors with tears in my eyes. I know what I'm crying about, but I'll write the story. Is why I'm writing the story.

I try to get back from my walk in the mornings before the traffic blocks up Saddle Road, or rather before the short-cutters start slicing their way off the Saddle Road higher up the valley and come through Fairways and fucking hinder my solitude and disturb the late sleeping Chief Justice on Golf Course View. Each morning now I've noticed that a black car with tinted windows is parked at the exit to his road. Took no notice the first two times, but now I've come to look out for it. Suspicious? They're an East Indian couple, middle-aged. One day from the corner of my eye I see that he has his head in her lap. Parking at this hour? Tender: he was like a baby wanting to suckle at her breast the way she held his head and looked down at him. The way he looked up at her. I wondered if they had just lost a child. Just a stray thought. What were they hiding?

T&T to the bone. Hug up me island. Rudder soca so sweet! Hug up me island!

Bear with me, Sas. You know it's fascinating how the security business has become real big business in such an unsafe place. Or so the talk is - because as I told these friends last night, you know, I'm a slow cruiser through the darkness of the darkest streets and all I can say is they are too fucking empty. Bravado, after two Merlots. Fear and dread eats the soul and everyone is behind their burglar proofing. Not the couple at dawn, easy to display their amorous rendezvous to me and the police who take no notice of them when they pass as dawn breaks and the white clouds turn to dun. P

Sasha is online. He replies right away:

What's dun, Pat?

Sas, it's pinkish brown. What's dun is done. Oh gawd! Bad eh? P

Sas, nothing is like the seventies when the boys hung out on the railings of Victoria Square and begged you to pick them up and life was civilised and poor and we weren't dying, being shot or kidnapped. Well, just so, say friends whom I can increasingly tell about my nightly sojourns - everyone is home because you can no longer walk the streets at night. And some PC jerk at More Vino, trendy wine bar on the waterfront, butts in with, 'Anyway, you'll fucking get HIV.' 'What?!' I scream and question. From driving around slowly at night because that is where I feel most comfortable rather than being locked up in my cage of an apartment, wondering what those poor kids are going through. Odd, and always interesting how homophobia manifests itself - often through guilt and self-loathing disguised as social responsibility. P

Pat, don't become too moralising, and watch yourself. I know this stuff is raw for you. S

The kids are all boys. Another one gone today. And none as yet found. The press keeps telling us the lurid stories of yesteryear because they don't have fresh blood. It isn't that I expect to find them out on empty streets playing or abandoned, or walking hand in hand with their abductor. I feel I need to have my finger on the pulse of this city, my beautiful belle d'Antilles. She, the city, is my femme fatale, my la diablesse, luring me into her darkness...

I fade out.

Take it easy, Pat. If you use too much of that kind of purple blood you'll lose your readers and yourself. Sas

What? Not too dark, Sas? Well what can I do with an insufferably romantic turn of mind and a burning anger for the things I love? Cynic, no, can't do cynic. What, like that fucker in More Vino? What does he understand about my desires? P

Cool it, Pat. Write your story, sweetheart. I love your romantic. Sas.

Are you worried about me, love? Condomise as they say here. No bareback. The latest attack is on Bi - big headlines about low-down and stealing a beautiful tender frame from Brokeback Mountain for their bigotry. Do people understand desire? Luv, P

I get the paper now after my walk from the fella outside Hi-Lo. And it's the usual thing, looking for the monster in a stranger when the statistics tell us that the monster is probably the big bad wolf in your parents' bed or your priest in the confessional.

There are security guards and three policemen at the school gates. I tried to get past them the other morning attempting to set up an interview with the headmistress. No dice. 'Miss Beaubrun just step out.' Keeping her head down. And the guards? Look what happened again the other day! Who is slipping through and how do they steal these boys?

I feed birds and I watch birds. Binoculars wonderful! And I must admit that when I'm watching the palm tanagers and my friend the one-legged tropical mockingbird, I'm taking in the arrivals and departures of the little boys in their khaki shorts and blue cotton shirts and their school bags bulging with libraries and sports' kits. The national flag unfurls itself in the wind from the school yard pole and the children pledge their pledge. Education! Was all part of a dream once in '62. I feel sick. Independence!

Doorbell. No one visits me. No one knows me. Is it a welcoming party? Callaloo and crab? Trinidad does not do welcoming parties. All of we is one! You know what I mean?

'I just wanted to say if you could mind how you feeding the birds because they does shit the pawpaw on my planter underneath.'

'Oh, sorry. I'm Patrice.' I put out my hand through the burglar proofing to shake the small hand of the delicate Indian lady from downstairs. 'I'm sorry. I'll stop feeding…'

'I'm Savi. And the water dripping from your air conditioner onto my louvres.'

'Oh dear, well…'

'I go get the fella in the yard to fix it. Run a PVC pipe…'

'Yes, anything. I'll pay.'

'Good. Have a nice day.'

'You, too. Excuse me. It's terrible isn't it….' But she had slipped down the stairs in the shadow of the palms on the landing. Then she called up sticking her head round the pillar.

'You like using your binoculars?' Then, like an afterthought as she flew, 'You shirt pretty eh?'

'Yes, you know…' But she was gone again, as swift as a hummingbird. I wondered what she thought of the disappearing little boys. I wanted to talk to people in the apartments. Someone must've noticed something. She's been keeping an eye on me.

I've forgotten with all the frantic emailing to mention

Carmella, my neighbour opposite on the same landing who amounted to a welcoming party - Chinese delicacies passed through a crack in my door the first morning. 'Thought you would like these.' Steamed wontons! Why not fried? I leave them for my lunch. Never saw her again for days except that I notice that every time I park my car under her window, she parts her curtains and looks out. Always at the window, peeping. I wonder what she's seen. Is she keeping an eye on me as well?

It's this one boy! He disappeared the day after I arrived in the apartment. Odd that the school has not been shut down. That would give me some peace but it might make it more difficult for me to learn anything. I still feel I will learn something as I sit here on mornings like James Stewart in *Rear Window* with Grace Kelly. Love those oldies with the stars. There's no Grace Kelly here. I wanted to be Grace Kelly once.

I sit with my binoculars, not lame like James Stewart. I stare into the assembly hall, keeping a watch on the main gate and playground. I train my binoculars on the tiptop flowering of the palmiste where the blue-grey tanagers and keskidees love to feed on the berries of the flowering Royal palm.

I had been doing this the morning after my arrival, when I saw him being picked up by a respectable-looking gentleman in a smart Rover. Not the most common car here, I thought, Japanese dominate with a variety of Nissans. The boy was black and also the gentleman, what I called old-fashioned political type, like the first crooks who stole all the oil money in the eighties. Of course, then I thought nothing of anything. It is only now, piecing together the stories, that I realise that I was probably the last to have seen him.

I phone Sasha: 'I think I was the last to see one of the little boys.' Then, I can't help myself.

'Take it easy, Pat. Come, come…'

I keep going over the moments and wondering what was in the frame which could tell me now that the man was or was not his father and if the little boy was at all anxious, resisting, being forced, some clue. I wish now it was not just the binoculars but the digital which I could have clicked away on and had the whole scene over and over to examine.

Sasha had given me the digital, bless him. But as you know, not like me to have any of that ready. Not like me at all. I have just bought my first mobile, cell. As I said, I'm stuck in the middle of the nineteenth century.

Patrice, it's been days! Where's my story? S

Sasha, as soon as I've got something you'll be the first to know. P.

I lie. *PS I'm very close now. P*

He doesn't reply. He's getting impatient.

I was entertaining myself with the daily opera, Australian Open over, and checking the gate and the playground when the doorbell went. Wontons? I could do with a Carmella visit. Shitting birds? Leaking air conditioner? Not Savi, please. I turned the lock, slid back the emergency chain, opened the door. Oh my God! The man in front of me carried what seemed like an enormous machine gun held almost pointing straight at me, but a little down to the ground when I looked again, catching my senses. I quickly wondered how he had gotten in at the foyer. Then that thought slipped away.

'Good morning, Sir,' he said.

'Morning officers?' I presumed that was what they were. There were two of them, standing one behind the other the other side of the padlocked burglar proofing. They looked like commando fighters, not police officers. This could have been a scene in Gaza.

'We would like to come in,' the front one said.

'What's this about?' I asked, reaching for the keys on the TV table, thinking this is quite extraordinary. And from somewhere, outrage, a feeling for my civil rights entered my head. I stopped reaching for the keys. 'Have you got a warrant?'

'We don't need a warrant, Sir. We just want to talk to you. If you refuse we'll go away and come back with a warrant and then it might be worse, you know.' He was losing his formality.

'You threatening me?'

'It won't be threats Sir, if we have to go and get a warrant, but we probably won't choose to do that. We can get through here quite easily, you know. Obstructing a police investigation does not improve your case.'

'Case? Which case? Is there a case? Talk to me from where you are, you don't have to come in.'

'Hiding something?' Then this first police officer standing closer to the gate turned to his partner and said, 'I wonder what they does have to hide? You have something you don't want we to see? We not going to interfere with you, you know.' You know, you know, it was like a nervous tic with this one, and the other one was smiling constantly, levelling his gun at me from time to time till he noticed and then pointing it at the ground again.

'Maybe he want us to interfere with him.' The one at the back laughed and they both laughed now. 'Look, open the focking gate eh! Sir. Or is it Madam?' I was terrified. The first one rattled the gate with the barrel of his gun. 'Open the focking gate you buller man!' I don't know where I got the strength or the nerve. I slammed the front door shut, bolted it and ran into my bedroom and shut that door too, imagining that I would have to lunge under the bed to escape the bullets following me through the door and ricocheting around the room. I had left the air conditioner on high and the room was as freezing cold as a morgue. I was terrified. I was sure they would blast themselves in. When that did not happen I knew they would be back with the warrant. What could I do?

There was a gentle knock at the door after what seemed like an eternity of silence and the muffled passing of traffic on Saddle Road. I thought if I looked outside I would see that it was snowing. I was that dislocated. I felt lonely, realised how isolated I was without any family here now. How had those brutes gotten into the compound and then into the foyer? And why me? And my address? I peeped through the glass peephole and saw a distorted Carmella with a plate of steamed wontons. I opened up.

'What going on?' She was a ministering angel.

'I don't know.' She came inside and sat on the sofa putting the plate of wontons on the coffee table. She was like a long-lost friend. The smell of the wontons pervaded the room. They looked like slabs of white flesh.

'Here, have a shot of brandy.' Carmella extracted from nowhere a small silver flask. It was metallic cold. I unscrewed the top and tipped the flask to my lips. I noticed that she was wearing a beautiful, red-silk kimono dressing gown. I was revived by the medicinal brandy. Carmella must've been very beautiful in her youth, she was ageless. She still dyed her hair

jet black. She could've been fifty-five or eighty. Then she said
gently without alarm, 'Now you see what the police are like
here. Them is part of the problem. How them could catch
bandits and kidnappers? Drink some more brandy. Eat a
wonton.' The brandy I sipped again, but the slabs of white
flesh revolted me. Their spicy smell going quickly stale, the
soya sauce sickly sweet.

'You have family, Patrice?'

'No, yes, all gone away. You know how it was? Black Power
1970. Parents bury in Lapeyrouse. Anyway...you know...'

'What you doing here then?'

'Love. Hug me island, hug me island.' I laughed.

'I see. You need somebody to help you, you know.'

Carmella advised me to call a lawyer. She got the phone
number of one she had once used. 'Her name is Jackie Sealy.
And don't worry with what them fellas tell you eh, don't worry
with them, their mind sick, oui.' She must've been lovely as a
young woman. I was reminded of *The World of Suzie Wong*.

When I asked her if she had noticed anything unusual
opposite she just said she didn't see too good. I didn't want to
quiz her, at least not at this moment. I was terrified. The police
could return at any moment. I called Jackie Sealy. She said I
should insist on a warrant and call her the moment they
arrived and she would be over for the interview. 'The way they
threatened and insulted you is not on,' she said. There was
goodness in the country, I thought.

As I waited for the police to arrive, it occurred to me that if
someone had seen me looking through the binoculars at the
school they might well have reported me as a suspect. That
thought made me sink deeper into the hammock. It was just
that way the morning after my arrival when I had seen him

arrive and depart and not thought anything of it - a little boy of ten or thereabouts getting into that Rover with a well-dressed gentleman whom I thought must be his dad, or even a minister of government. No, they're too smooth, dressed up in their big suits as if against the cold, and go off in tinted cars which break the vehicle regulations. Anyway, black on black?

'What does that mean?' Sasha asked when he phoned. Trying not to worry him, I explained that people had theories that crime here was committed by black people on Indians. I told him I had no evidence of that. Did anyone? Evidence was not what people needed to believe something like that here, just a racist mind.

'Watch how you put any of that.'

When the police returned they were quite different in manner. They had their warrant to search and interview. I told them I was instructed to call my lawyer and they accepted. My suspicion was that they were doing everything by the book because they really thought they were onto something, a serial paedophile, and if they messed up because of procedure they would have no case.

The crunch came after the formalities and in the middle part of the interview. Jackie scrutinised them and examined every phrase in their questions. I felt so safe with her there. This would be such a good bit for my story. I had a small tape running that I used for my research with an omni mic. I might not get everything but it would be wonderful to get even the scraps of this interview and the noises as they opened and closed cupboards and doors. I knew that if Jackie weren't here there would have been obscenities. I had flicked on the tape just before they arrived. They missed it in their cursory search of the lounge, they were so obsessed with my bedroom and my clothes' cupboard and drawers where I kept my underwear and socks. I watched them snigger over my jocks and briefs. Don't think the tape got that, more raising of their eyebrows and nasty smirks. Jackie for a moment was on her cell. They were even in the dirty clothes' basket. They had those white gloves which they slipped on. I thought of condoms as they inserted their large black fingers. An erotic thought allowed me to escape my fear. One of the guys was very good looking and sexy in his uniform with all the gadgetry of arrest and constriction hanging off him. If I were going to write sado this would be where I would have to begin.

'Do you have a pair of binoculars?'

'Yes.' They had picked them up in the search so I don't know why they were asking me. Jackie whispered that they had to do their job this way. That was fine. She was almost holding my hand.

'Do you use them?'

'Yes.'

'Did you use them this morning?'

'Yes.'

'For what purpose?'

'Bird watching.'

'There is a witness ready to testify that you were seen training your binoculars on the school opposite.'

'Yes, I do look at the school opposite.'

'For what purpose?'

'It's unavoidable really. Birds fly where they will.' I said this with a flourish of my hand.

'This is a criminal investigation, Sir. We expect you to take our questions seriously.'

'My client is taking your questions seriously,' Jackie interjected. She smiled at me encouragingly. 'You can put the question again, Officer.'

'Very well. For what purpose did you have your binoculars trained on the school and the school children?'

'Well, seriously it is unavoidable when looking at birds as you can imagine, but yes, I thought I would do a bit of detection. We're all aware of what's going on. There doesn't seem to be too much detection going on in this country.' And prosecutions, well…' I could hear my voice getting excitable. Jackie was warning me with her eyes.

'I would caution you, Sir, to answer the questions appropriately otherwise we will have no choice but to charge you with obstructing our legitimate police investigation into the abduction of a number of children from Miss Beaubrun's school.'

'You might make better use of your time trying to find the abductors and the children and that little boy rather than wasting your time interviewing me.'

'Sir, I caution you.'

'My client apologises, Officer. It won't happen again.' I could see that Jackie was saying this to me. Jackie was a smart young black woman trained at the local law school. Carmella said she was the best in town.

'What do you mean, that little boy?' the officer asked. The room was as silent as a tomb. The glass doors to the verandah were closed, but at that moment you could hear the cries of children from the school opposite. It was recess. Jackie looked at me. I looked at her and we both looked at the officers sitting opposite. It was fear. It was some intractable part of my unconscious, some memory I could never remember. My memory expressed itself as tears that welled up in my eyes and ran down my cheeks. I expect the officers thought, *He's cracking up, we'll get a confession any moment.* Jackie looked pretty apprehensive as if saying what haven't you told me. She got me a glass of water and a Kleenex from her bag. It smelt of some kind of Chanel. Gradually, I pulled myself together and spoke.

'One of them. The day after I first came back I was doing what I told you, bird watching. I saw that little boy, the one who disappeared on the 20th of November. I've been reading the reports. I feel sure it was he that I saw get into a Rover with a well-dressed gentleman. It was mid-morning when I have a break and I thought it odd that the boy was leaving school then, but other than that I did not think anything because at that time I did not know about the abductions, having just come back into the country. But piecing together the stories in the papers I feel pretty sure.'

'Why all the interest?' This question was spontaneous and not one of their prepared questions.

'I write. I'm writing a story about the disappearing children for a journal in London.'

'But you've been withholding information in a criminal investigation. Why didn't you report this?'

Jackie was looking intently at me. I had not told her this.

'When I first saw him I was unaware of the abductions. When I found out, my visit to the police station did not inspire confidence. You fellas don't have a good press.'

'I would not play detective, Sir. And now to clear you from our list of suspects we will require you to come down to the Saint Claire police station and give us your fingerprints and other particulars.' Jackie nodded. This was appropriate formality.

'Yes, certainly. But you know when you came earlier, even

today when you were going through my private things...'

'If you or your lawyer has any complaints, Sir, you can put them in writing to the Commissioner of Police. You understand? You know.' There it was again, you know. That nervous tic. That told me that they had got to their limit of good behaviour. The fuckers. They were going to get away with their obscenity and brutality.

'One thing, Sir. We would like an item of clothing from your soiled clothes to match a stain there with other evidence.'

'You what?' It was all in his eyes, the hate, the brutality which he had not been able to administer.

Jackie was utterly professional. 'I trust that the item of clothing will be returned to my client in the proper manner.' They did not bother to reply, so Jackie repeated the question.

'Yeah, man,' the officer replied.

'Officer, I will repeat my question again and I will expect you to take the matter of a criminal investigation seriously. I trust that the item of clothing will be returned to my client in the proper manner.'

'Yes, Madam.' Jackie went down to the police station with me and the officer on duty did the required.

Weeks have gone and I've not made any headway with my little boy or with my weight despite the fact that I am walking each day. Walk faster, eat less. How will I make the road on j'ouvert morning?

I get these ideas into my head on my walks. I have been noticing this house, cute little bungalow, just round the corner really with petreas which have just burst into bloom, bluey purple; gorgeous colour and I love that I know the names of trees. The house is empty, or looks like it is. I wonder about that each morning as I pass and dream. I have been building a fantasy that I would love to give up my cage and move into this bungalow. I can see that there is a garden behind. The porch has been closed in, pity, fear!

I'm still shaken by my visitation from the police. I keep my focus. No, not on my childhood, my stolen childhood, but the stolen childhoods which are at the moment plaguing this city.

I think the teachers are having a meeting today. No kids have arrived. That's ominous. I hope now that they are not going to close the school though I completely understand why if they do. What have I got? Absolutely nothing. We need detection. Do you know that DNA is not allowed as evidence in the attempt to prosecute in this country? What are they going to do with my soiled briefs?

There he is. I can see him. He's running along the pavement opposite - khaki pants, blue shirt, satchel for a mountain climber on his back, a mite stacked with education books and his mum's and dad's hopes and ambitions, not to mention Miss Beaubrun's injunctions based on the national anthem where every creed and race find an equal place, and as it was just Christmas time when I came, the carols of the story of Bethlehem. What I think is that every creed and race does have an equal place and that any of them could be the abductor of the children, of my little boy. He has a name. His name is Elijah.

Sas. Can you imagine the weight of that name in a country that not only needs a prophet but a promised land to go to? No, fucking hell no! Not any more of those. Can't we just stay here and clean up the shit we've got? Sas, how cynical can I get. P

There he is, the smallest boy of ten that you can imagine. He is skipping alongside the gentleman. I take it to be his father. It's a dream. I'm that obsessed. It's just that he looks like I looked at ten in khaki pants and blue shirt. A disappeared childhood. I once said I loved my childhood.

The couple, each morning parked just below the Chief Justice's house in the ferny gulch with the bamboos, are there again today. Sas, they were having a row this morning. Where do they fit in? Still suspicious. Then I notice that the house, the cute bungalow, has two cars parked underneath. One is a Nissan Sunny, can't make out the other. Oh no, someone has bought my bungalow. There's a lot of garbage out this morning, stacks of old newspapers and several black plastic bags. They're moving in? Moving out? P

'You feeling OK?' Carmella asks through the burglar proofing when she hands me her weekly delivery of steamed wantons.

'You want to come in?'

'You want company.' She tells me, sitting on the sofa, that despite her bad eyesight she remembers that she did notice the Rover. 'You know why?'

'No?'

'I had an old man friend who used to drive one and come and take me out. He died this year. I get accustom looking out of the window when I hear a car arrive to park under the window. Next to your place is my place but I don't have a car. He used to park there.'

'I'm sorry.'

Odd light today. When this happens everyone says it's Sahara dust. The Harmattan! A dusty wind across the Middle Passage.

When I come back down from the hills after my walk, past the couple in their car, I notice that one of the cars from the cute bungalow is parked outside on the road. It's a Rover. My heart misses a beat. The windows and windscreen are caked with dust and someone has scrawled something in the Sahara dust at the bottom of the back right-hand side window. Because it's just by me I stop to read, to decipher, because the dew, like tears has smudged the message. It's just one word, two - Elijah Help.

I do my duty and call the police on my cell.

We're too late.

Sas, this is a dark time, my love. The bodies of the boys have been found. A boy of twelve was drowned in a pond. The autopsy revealed sexual assault. Another boy was raped, rupturing his internal organs. Another two boys were found raped. The boy named Elijah was buggered, beaten and tortured. The owner of the Rover was picked up, but without DNA will he be prosecuted? The Minister for National Security, speaking on crime in the country, said that free education had been given, unemployment was down, the economy was buoyant: youth were not availing themselves of these opportunities and they had lost sight of God. People should pray.
Well, how much darker can we get than this, Sas? P

Phone me. Sas

The Penalty of Death

The wheel-chair was parked at the bottom of the stairs. Curdella Marvel avoided bumping into it as she came in from the pantry through the living room to open up Doreen Handle's house that morning. 'Cheups, that confounded chair.' This was a daily routine, a daily complaint. She knew that, particularly this morning, she had to avoid annoying Miss Handle by bumping into the chair. Everything had to go like clockwork this morning, as Miss Handle, Judge Handle, got ready for court. This was the day that they had been waiting for these last three months.

Curdella passed a duster over the furniture as she sashayed through the room, making her way towards the large verandah doors. She checked the pink and white anthurium lilies, which stood against the creamy walls, their long stems steeped in the cool water of the deep vase. She would have to change the water. She could detect that mossy smell Miss Handle could not abide. 'So many confounded flowers, it does smell like a funeral parlour in here sometimes, yes.' Curdella kept her voice down. She kept her complaints to herself. The early morning breeze off the verandah filled the room through the latticed doors, which she had just unlatched, hooking their backs to the wall, so that they would not bang later on when a wind, or a sudden gust, before heavy rain, might play hurricane-havoc with the interior decor of Miss Handle's home.

The spacious high-ceilinged room was L-shaped. The vertical of the L was the dining room with its long table and eight chairs. This room was complete with a glass cabinet filled with Miss Handle's crystal. 'I just love any kind of cut glass. It quite excites me, always has. Since I'm a girl. Like Mother.' Curdella had had to listen for years to these effusive declarations when she served at Miss Handle's dinner parties. She had witnessed her growing up in this very house. The room now reflected her idea of elegance and achievement. 'So much furnitures, and this blasted polished floor. One day I go have to tell her she need to bring some able-bodied young girl from the village to do this work. I not able now. You see me, is justice I want, yes.'

She continued with her dusting. She had to take particular care with this other arrangement, two silver, oval-framed portraits of Miss Handle's mother and father in sepia when they were in their forties. Gertrude and George Handle stared out formally from their studio portraits into the family home, which was now their daughter's. 'These were people. They knew how to treat a servant.' Curdella did not like the term, servant. She preferred, housekeeper. Though, if she were honest with herself, and not giving into her complaints, she knew that she had been more of a servant to Mr and Mrs Handle, and now, a very needed housekeeper to their daughter, the young judge.

She had to treat the portraits with reverence. You might want to genuflect there, as at an altar, light a candle. Certainly, for Miss Handle, it was one of the places at which she was reminded to pray for them, and for that reason, Curdella made sure that everything on that table was kept perfectly dusted and polished.

As she performed this sacred duty, she picked up the

portraits and admired her previous master and mistress. Mr Handle was distinguished in a brown suit of the 1930s period. He wore glasses that gave him a serious look. Mrs Handle also wore glasses and this added to her handsome femininity a certain rigour. 'Madam, was nice, yes, when she was younger. Look what old age do to she now.' There was a contrast between the soft folds of her ivory collar and sleeves, reminding one of a younger woman who was once innocent, and the knowing look, which came from behind the eyes. 'What old age do to she, but she not give up yet. But look the boss, so handsome as he used to be. The Lord Jesus take him early. Don't know when He coming for she.' Curdella rested the portraits down carefully.

While George Handle had been a judge, his wife had chaired many social committees. Her major work was with The Society for the Betterment of Young Coloured Women and The Society for the Eradication of Poverty. Curdella knew that she had been rescued from the poverty of her mother's overcrowded board house by this good woman and her husband. She was proud of how some of her people had progressed in life. But that did not mean, she thought this morning, as she did on many mornings, that she should still have to be doing this work now that she was so elderly herself. This was not justice. She would have to get some justice for herself before she died.

Doreen Handle had continued to lie in bed. She liked the sunlight to wake her. As the long white cotton drapes sailed forth from the window with the morning breeze, the day began to collect around her. Immediately, the cares of the day began to tighten around her. They were a hand clenched on her heart, in a tight fist. She had dreaded this day, had seen it coming these last three months during the trial of the young man, Christian Manners.

She could hear Curdella in the kitchen with the clatter of breakfast. She heard when her footsteps disappeared and when they returned to the soft tread of the floorboards of the dining room and the carpeted floor of the living room. Curdella was now ready to climb the stairs and, as so often happened, and as she had tried earlier to avoid doing, she bounced into the wheel-chair parked near the small bookcase at the foot of the stairs.

'Curdella child, watch you foot on that wheel-chair,' Doreen called out through the bedroom door which was always left open now.

'Yes, Miss Handle.' Then the wheel-chair rolled and bounced again against the small bookcase.

'Oh, Curdella!' Doreen sat up, fretting to herself, staying at the side of her bed for a moment's meditation, swinging her bare feet onto the wooden floor. 'Curdella?'

'What you say Miss Handle? Sorry Miss Doreen, I know is today...'

'Curdella, just keep your mind on your work, and I will keep my mind on what I have to do.'

'I pray for that fella last night, you know. The quality of mercy is not strained, it droppeth as the gentle rain from heaven upon the place beneath.'

'Curdella, what you talking about at this hour of the morning? Quoting Shakespeare, child!'

'And is so that gentleman, your father, teach me. I watching him this morning on the table in the drawing room, and wondering what he would have tell you if he was here to advise you.' Curdella's voice was now sounding like the young girl she must have been when Father taught her to read the famous extract from *The Merchant of Venice*, and to perform it in the church hall with the appropriate gesticulations, expressions he thought that her Portia should possess.

The two women were now shouting to be heard, one from the edge of her bed the other from the foot of the stairs.

'Curdella, you better get my breakfast on time today.'

'Yes, Miss Doreen.'

Doreen sat and listened as her housekeeper, a woman who had been her nurse since she was a little girl, retreated into the pantry, bouncing once more into the wheel-chair. 'She will never learn. What to do?'

Since the morning that the wheel-chair was first delivered, Doreen, like Curdella, did not like the look of it. It stood there, incongruously, on the gravel yard, taken down from the delivery van. 'What kind of thing is this?' Curdella asked if this was right and proper for Mrs Handle. 'You going and strap you mother into this chair? What we coming to now?'

Doreen had agreed silently with Curdella, and had always thought that there was something eerie about the way the rubberised wheels glided over the tiles of the verandah, and ran smoothly across the polished floorboards, giving off the slightest jangle, as a collection of its accoutrements, straps and buckles hit against the chrome arm rests as it hiccupped over the soft hump of her Wilton carpet to rest with a small reverberating bump against the legs of a nest of tables. It had got out of hand then as it had continued to do every morning. She did find it difficult to believe that Curdella could really be bumping into it every morning, after being repeatedly warned about it. Perhaps the chair had a life of its own? She used to ask herself if it was, in fact, bumping into Curdella, who had perhaps found that too unbelievable to report; too macabre, maybe. Doreen did not like the feel of its silver chrome. She did not like the black leatherette seat and back rest. When she first sat in it to try it out herself, it sent a shiver down her spine. The cold chrome repelled her. She hated the feeling; a sinking sensation in the pit of her stomach when she strapped herself in, negotiating the difficult contraption of the movable foot rests. She felt hemmed in.

Seeing it standing there, that morning, in the yard, then being rolled into the house, filled her with dread. Curdella was right. But how else was she to move her mother? Neither of them could be constantly lifting her.

Doreen, pulling her housecoat about herself, met Curdella at the top of the stairs with a tray of breakfast that was brought up each morning at this time for Gertrude Handle. 'Is OK Curdella, give me the tray. Continue with my breakfast. Just eggs, don't worry with the buljol.'

'And I soak the salt fish since I get up early, especially, yes.'

'Curdella. Don't fuss. I've got to be in court early today. Give me the tray. I'll see to Mother myself.'

'I know. I thinking about you, you know. An upright judge, a learned judge.'

'Curdella! Thank you, Curdella.'

Doreen entered her mother's room off the landing at the top of the stairs. She had taken to sleeping with her mother. But because she had not done so last night, she felt guilty. Gertrude Handle, Mother, lay perilously close to the edge of the bed. Doreen always wondered how she had never fallen off. But that was where she preferred to lie for the entire night. Her will had not diminished, but her body was extremely frail. As her frame had shrunk, her head seemed bigger. Her eyes opened wide and lit up, a life burning out fast, galloping towards its own end. It was all in her eyes. The body was weak. She was ninety-eight years old.

'Morning, Mother.' The morning sun was already burning its way through the floral cotton curtains. As Doreen pushed them aside, the radiance of the light blinded her and swept across the polished wooden floor and startled her mother, causing her to open her eyes even more and turn her head slowly towards her daughter. She did not say anything. She looked and gestured with her hand and her outstretched index finger, with which she jabbed imperiously the edge of the bed beside her. This meant that Doreen should come and sit next to her.

As Doreen sat on the slither of mattress, which was left, her mother pulled at the sleeve of her housecoat and partly sat up. She licked her lips and moistened them. Opening her eyes wider than ever, she said, 'That man you are going to execute this morning, are you sending him to the chair?'

For a moment, Doreen did not understand what her mother was saying. It was so unexpected, this first utterance. It was true that early morning was her most lucid time. Later, as the day progressed, and she grew more tired, dream and reality, the distant past and the recent past merged into surprising juxtapositions with present events.

'What you saying, Mother?'

'Christian Manners, the fella you've been talking about these last few months.'

It was true, that after work on some afternoons, Doreen would come home and lie next to her mother and talk through her day. But she never thought that her mother was taking it all in. Certainly, she did not think that she would remember it for long or worry over a particular point, bring it up so lucidly in the morning on just awakening from a long night's rest, on the very morning that Doreen had to go to court to pronounce a judgement on the young man, Christian Manners from Hope Village; she had recently discovered, or rather, came to realise this was the same Hope Village that she always drove through on the way to Brenda's, her dear friend who had kept her sane during the long trial.

'Yes, Mother, Christian Manners. What about the boy?'

'A boy? I saw him. A young man, big and strong like those young fellas that come in the yard to mow the lawns and cut the hedges, wearing them cut off pants and cloth tied round their head.'

'A boy, Mother. OK, yes, a young man. You saw him? How you could see him? Where?'

'Yes, I definitely saw him.' The index finger jabbed at the springs in the mattress beneath the sheets. 'In the electric chair?'

'Mother, we hang here, we don't use the electric chair. That is what they use in America, in some states, but not here. You know that!'

'He was in the chair.' Gertrude Handle was now sitting bolt upright in bed and continuing to jab her finger forcefully on the bed beside her. 'I did see him. He was sitting in the chair, strapped in. Like you do to me.'

'Mother, what are you saying? You must have dreamt that. It's a wheel-chair, not an electric chair. I don't strap you into an electric chair.' Doreen was horrified by her mother's dream. It must have been a dream. What else? A hallucination? She was sure it was the new tablets her mother had been given by Dr Lamming that were playing tricks with her mind.

Doreen had once thought, after resting with her mother one afternoon after work and unburdening herself of her day, what it must have sounded like. What it might have sounded like, to say, Curdella, if she had been the listener. It would not have been at all appropriate for Curdella to hear her analysis of the day's proceedings in court. She could read the reports in the paper. But there she would not have read the judge's thoughts and reflections. She would not have read of the judge's fears. These she told to her mother, a listener, as in a Roman Catholic confessional. It was like talking to someone who would never bring it up, would not be hearing it like ordinary people listen. Mother was the perfect confessor because she would almost immediately forget. 'Mother. I must get dressed. Don't fret yourself.'

'You going out today and leaving me?'

'Mother, you know I have to go out. Curdella will be with you. Eat your breakfast, while I get dressed.'

As Doreen got ready, she was more distracted than ever. She took even more care with the sobriety of her dress this morning, knowing that the press would be outside the courthouse. While this case had been her very particular concern, her mother's state of mind was something that also obsessed Doreen in these latter days of her caring for her mother. It seemed an eternity that she had been lying in that bed. Yet, she could not imagine it any differently. Mother's memory was even more scrambled than ever, like the other day when she got back from the court.

'My God, there you are. You're OK. I got Curdella to call the office, but they said you had already left. Have you no scratches? Have you not broken something?'

'Curdella?' She had turned to Curdella.'What is Mother talking about? You called my office? About what?'

'She wouldn't settle down Miss Handle till I phone the office and ask what happen in the crash.'

'For pity's sake!! What crash? What on earth are you talking about?'

At this point, her mother, unusually, shouted out. 'The one in Tel Aviv. Did you not know where you were?'

'Mother, I've been in town all day in court until I flew into my office to pick up some papers on my way home this afternoon. What on earth have you and Curdella been watching on the television? Curdella, I thought I told you not to put my Mother through your matinee viewing. If you have to watch those terrorising movies, go downstairs and watch them on the big television screen. I'm going to get you and Mother some nice gentle nature films to watch together in the day when I'm not here. If she wants to see me strolling in some meadow in Vermont that would be preferable to her seeing me as a victim in a plane crash in Tel Aviv.'

Curdella was correct earlier this morning. Doreen needed her father at this moment as she drove to the courthouse to pronounce the sentence in a case that had disturbed her because of its deep complexities. It had scandalised the whole island. It was a while since her father had passed over. She was not quite sure how she imagined him in that other place, if she imagined him at all. It was just a sense of him that she had, a kind of memory, and a kind of hope.

She was just approaching Hope. She came this way to see her friend Brenda, in the hills at the centre of the island, and it was her short cut to avoid the traffic on the highway. She felt that that she had always had hope. It sustained her in her life. As she drove along the narrow, rough road through the sugarcane, the Indian jhandis on their bamboo poles caught the wind. Prayers carried by the flags on the breeze, she thought, as she reached the brow of the hill overlooking Hope.

The village had been heralded from a distance by a row of tall Royal palms; their trunks 'like Doric columns of ancient Greece' as she had once read in one of her school books, *West Indian Summer*. Was that *Charles* Kingsley, one of the nineteenth-century travellers to the islands?

She could understand naming the place, Hope. As she drove nearer and came to the little barrack rooms set in a higgledy-piggledy collection around the old sugar factory, she felt that the name, Hope, had carried the aspirations of the villagers in their confinement, of her own enslaved people, the proletariat, now in a free and independent nation. Hope. She could hear the aspiration of her parents and then of herself in the casuarinas tossed by the wind.

Hope, a small word, was a large prayer in the mind and on the lips of Doreen Handle this morning. She thought of Christian Manners. She had to keep a clear head.

Doreen neared the court and could see the gathering paparazzi, as these vultures were called abroad. Her mind was still on the wheel-chair and her mother's grotesque image of herself strapped into an electric chair. Someone had told her once that a wheel-chair was a godsend.

Come to think of it, that was the same expression one of her colleagues had made in connection with reference to the electric chair over lunch the other day, discussing the relative advantages and disadvantages of the various methods of capital punishment. 'The chair is a godsend, man. We should get one. I think it would seem less barbaric than the gallows. Maybe that is what people are reacting to, those against hanging.' Doreen never liked her smart-arsed - she allowed herself the apt expression - colleague, Anil Maharaj, recently out from law school in England. His comment now sent a chill down her spine, reminding her of her mother's accusation earlier this morning.

Pulling into her parking bay, having escaped the press, she counted to herself that she had sent three men to the gallows over the years. She had always known what would be expected of her judgements once the law and the constitution had to be upheld. She had been quietly relieved when the death sentence had been suspended for a trial period. She was upset when they had restored it.

What kind of society were we Doreen asked herself? The Christian Manners case had been worrying her since all the controversy over crime and punishment. Was it true that over eighty percent of the population wanted to retain hanging? Was that the way for the politicians to view law making? She heard Curdella's voice, 'The quality of mercy is not strained...' as she heard her entrance announced into the courtroom. 'All stand...'

Driving home that afternoon, she made a detour to Brenda's. She had called her earlier. 'I need a stiff drink, girl, a good rum.' Her people, what had happened to her people, she asked herself as she drove towards the blue hills in the declining light of late afternoon?

Along the way, the churches multiplied, appearing between the Hindu mandirs and Muslim mosques. They seemed to be the most productive industry in this time of recession. There was the Church of the Nazarene, on the corner by Sam's Bakery. Just down the road, there was the Cathedral of the People and The Assembly of the Lord. It frightened her that all were preaching a vengeful God. The tears were streaming down her face. She hoped no smart-arsed young journalist that expression again - was on a motorbike following her an interview and a story. She could hardly see through the rear-view mirror, blurred by her tears.

She remembered her father telling her of when he had had to witness a hanging and he had described the look on the face of the condemned man, the look on the face of the man who had administered the execution. Grey despair. She had wondered about the look on his own face. He had left the chamber and been sick on the floor outside. She heard again her voice in court pronouncing judgement.

'What kind of society are we creating?' Doreen sobbed on her cell phone to Brenda. 'All we seem to read in newspapers are accounts of lurid murders and executions. What effect is that having on how we live? We are becoming obsessed with killing. Our pretty island is a killing field.'

As she neared Brenda's, she entered Hope Village. By now she had calmed down from her rant. Don't drive and speak on your cell, she told herself. Christian Manners: the boy had been looking at her from the dock for these last three months. He was a boy, despite the bravado of his posture, his developed physique. He was a soft-eyed child, despite the horror of what he had done. She had never seen a seasoned killer in his face.

Hope, she loved this pretty village, the way the frangipani hung over the fences on the corner when she took the turning up to Brenda's. Hope was a Christian virtue. She prayed for it. It was something she needed as she faced her mother's death. At ninety-eight she could not live much longer. What kind of hope did Christian Manners ever have? What hope now before early tomorrow morning? She knew the prison pastor was seeing him. Yet, he had not shown any remorse.

She stopped on the brow of the hill, got out of the car and looked down into the barrack yards. This was where the almost mythic act had been committed. This is what she saw each day as she listened to the trial unfold in court. The young boy, the son, had come upon his mother bent over a wash tub and chopped her with a cutlass once, and then when she had turned towards him, he struck another blow across her chest, slicing through her breasts, and then, when she had fallen, he had attacked her two screaming daughters, his sisters, and brought them to the ground.

Doreen stared into the distance beyond the yards across the island and let the re-enactment work on her in the heat and haze of distance with the wind blowing the sugarcane and the voices from the yards, small children's voices, rising up. There was a clang of iron coming from the old factory. It reminded her of the tolling of a bell. Yes, cane was bitter.

Christian Manners, Doreen meditated on the name. It was as if in his very name he had been branded with her people's history. Customs were named within his name. His name memorialised lives and ritualised deaths and unrecorded burials. His first name echoed the baptism of his people in the Christian faith, their heathen ways civilised by the priest with his cupped hand at the font, at the front of those churches dotted over the island. How had they coupled their colonial enterprise with the Christian faith? His surname, Manners, what a wonderful name. Doreen loved manners, good manners. 'The child must have manners.' She heard her mother's voice since she was a little girl. The name must have come from an English family, like one that used to live in that house just there among the Royal palms. Doreen had a view of an old estate house on a morne above the factory, a Great House.

A speeding car screamed passed her, coming along the narrow road. These young people, she thought, were helping to create the drug problem she had before her in the courts every day. She stood beside her car in the wake of the churned up dust of the disappearing car. Manners, the family name must have been passed down to an outside child, or taken by the enslaved. The name re-enacted the brutal and brutalising history of the island.

Christian Manners, he must have been teased at school, Doreen smiled. With such a name, it was an intelligent tease.

Sitting on Brenda's beautiful verandah looking out to the sea in the distance, they talked. 'Is this what it is to be made in the image and likeness of God?' Doreen asked Brenda.

'Child, have another rum. These things bigger than us.'

'But why I doing this work?'

'Because sometimes you do good. You speak out for change. But it need more than one voice.'

'Like for all the other things we have to change, we need more than one voice.'

Then, the rain came down.

Doreen drove home, leaving Hope behind her with its flickering lights, like fireflies on the verge. She knew that she would soon have to bear the penalty of her mother's death. Would her death be a release? Had she done enough for her mother?

Doreen slept with Mother that night. Her terror would not let go of her dreams. She was sure that what she had heard was the sound of the wheel-chair bumping into the bookcase at the bottom of the stairs. The house was secure. She had never really feared a burglar. Curdella would not be wandering into the house at this hour of the night. She decided to go downstairs and make herself a hot drink to help her back to sleep, one of those soothing herbal teas.

When she got to the bottom of the stairs, she saw that the wheel-chair was in the middle of the drawing room with its back to her. She recognised him at once, even though she could not see his face. As he moved his head, his locks shook out over his shoulders like the tresses of a young girl. He had claimed Rastafarianism when they wanted to cut his hair in prison. Suddenly, he swivelled round and faced her. He was strapped into the wheel-chair and there was a long lead running to where the stereo was plugged in. He held in his hand one of those switches on the cord. As he continued to stare at her, he pressed the switch. He went into spasm, the current searing through his arms, legs and brain.

Doreen woke suddenly, disturbed, she thought, by her mother. 'What is it Mother?'

'I see him again in the wheel-chair.'

'Is OK, Mother. Just a dream.'

She lay back down. She thought she smelt burning. She got up and went into her own room. Curdella had been up very early, doing the ironing. When she got back into the bed alongside her mother, Doreen reflected on her own dream, her own terror, seeing Christian Manners in the wheel-chair electrocuting himself. She remembered also that she had not told her mother of the judgement she had passed.

When she woke later in the morning, next to her mother, Doreen heard Curdella coming up the stairs. She met her on the landing with Mother's breakfast tray.

'So, they get their pound of flesh? They get their justice? I read it in the papers.' Curdella handed over the tray.

'More than that, girl, much more than that. We kill our hope.'

'Hope?'

'Yes, hope. Our hope lies in the lives of those young men shooting and knifing each other every murdering day.'

The rain was still falling, Curdella's voice faded away as she recited, 'It droppeth as the gentle rain from heaven upon the place beneath.' She paused at the top of the stairs.

'Mercy?'

'Mercy, yes, and hope too. But is justice tempered with that mercy, as your father used to say, that we need.'

'His generation was wise.'

'Is buljol today for you, yes. I buy the salt fish early this morning in the market. Four o'clock catch me down town.'

'You are a marvel, yes, Curdella. You know that, don't you? Let me give Mother her breakfast.'

Mercy

The girl had the weekend off.

Sybil left the house after putting the pot of split-pea soup to boil slowly on the kerosene stove. She left the rice simmering.

Jonathan could not find his mother behind the pall of dark filling the recesses of the porch, the drawing room, dining room and the four bedrooms where he now wandered frantically in from play. Where was she?

'Mummy,' he cried, fleeing the dark corridor from the bedrooms, nothing familiar in his fear. He feared the kitchen's night before the Delco lights brought their weak orange glow, the colour of rum, to the lamps of the cavernous bungalow. 'Mummy!'

The ultimate fear had not quite descended, it being still that brief twilight when the east side of the house was all in shadow, so that he could not even see his mother's tuberoses, which were like the ones in St Joseph's arms in the chapel of the Holy Innocents down the hill. Nor could he see the clumps of palms, which were sinister and looked like jumbies; no longer the hiding places for a child's games in the bright sunshine of the daytime.

All was still in shadow before the transient miracle of fireflies on the gravel avenue of casuarinas which ended in what his mother called eternity.

Neither was she under the house, where that labyrinth of wire clothes' lines with still damp washing, sheets and clammy, long khaki pants his father wore for work, still hung.

Then he heard the crunch on the gravel.

Sybil had already gone. The watchman had not as yet come. He turned, saw nothing, but continued to hear the rhythmic pace; its ongoing meditation into what he was sure was eternity. Footsteps, like in 'O'Grady says...'

The west side of the house was battered with the last of the shattering sunset which illuminated the sky over the gulf and undulating sugarcane fields of Endeavour estate like a canvas depicting creation, or God Almighty coming down from heaven on Judgement Day.

His mother was not there, not part of that illumination. Where was she? 'Mummy.'

The crunch on the gravel was on the other side of the house in the shadows and the increasing darkness. He didn't know who it was.

Down the gravel gap he saw the last of the nurses making their way home to the overseers' bungalows, pushing their prams and pulling along their toddlers. He heard their cries, and the little ones breaking away for one last game of 'Brown girl in the ring, Tra la la la la...She looks like a sugar in a plum plum plum...'; the little ring of children in best frocks and sun-suits singing.

'Mummy, Mummy, where are you?' He hoped that his cry from where he was hidden would reach her, wherever she was, even though he was lost for a moment amid the clammy washing, which, except for the damp, his mother liked to call the hole of hell, or the black hole of Calcutta, preferring the nurses to go down there.

Hell smelt of oil where his father's Land Rover dripped at the entrance onto the concrete. But, it smelt mostly of washing and scrubbing boards and tubs with blue soap and Mercy's body, bent like a crooked stick over the ironing board. Mercy could not bend her legs. She stood stock-still on them. She had to raise them one by one to walk as if they were perpetually in splints. Had she tried to heed the words of the gospel? 'Take up your bed and walk, and come follow me.' She walked like this every weekday from Hope Village along the pitch road in the heat, and then up the gravel gap from the Chiney shop to do the washing and the ironing at the manager's house of Endeavour estate. She could not get up the back stairs and so was sentenced to the thraldom of hell, or the black hole of Calcutta, both for work and her breakfast of bread and butter and hot cocoa-tea. Here she left her smell, her work clothes hanging on a rusty nail. 'Nigger-sweat,' the child had heard others call it. Sweat and blue soap. There was the smell of ironing on damp clothes and starch still sticky in an old chipped, blue-rimmed, enamel basin. Light into hell came through the west latticework, which filtered in streams of God's creation setting.

Still, he could not find his mother. 'Mummy, Mummy, where are you?'

'Darling, I'm here.' And, for a moment, it sounded like she was playing hide-and-seek with him. 'Come and get me I'm here, hiding in the clumps of palms', which he was sure had now completely disappeared, or turned into those whispering presences he saw out of his bedroom window when he looked out before getting into bed to check that no one from the barrack rooms was shinnying up the bathroom pipes to steal or murder.

His father refused to believe that coolies could break into the house. Though they, the grown ups, said, 'Can't trust a coolie,' when they clinked ice in glasses of rum and soda on evenings when the sun went down and uncles and aunts came to visit from the town, or now and then, English people from the company, came for drinks, 'Trust a nigger any day, lazy breed, but never trust a coolie.'

There were no visitors this evening.

Jonathan followed the direction of his mother's voice away from the crunch on the gravel, wondering about those O'Grady steps which went on and on into eternity, coming back on themselves. Could you do that? Go into eternity and come back? Jesus was coming back to take us all into himself, the blue penny catechism said. But now he only wished his mother would be there where he could find her.

Her voice came from the kitchen and he ventured through the pantry into the darkness. 'Where are you? Where are you?'

'My pet.'

Then he found her standing over the stove.

'The girl's off for the weekend.' She was standing over a pot of split-pea soup, stirring. Rice was boiling away in another pot. He went and stood beside her, feeling safe after the run back from the Eccles where he played after school.

'Where's Dad?'

She continued to stir, and then she looked at him, and then at the dirty wall of the kitchen. 'He's outside, poor dear, wrestling with the devil.' Jonathan heard the crunch on the gravel.

She stirred and he continued to stand next to her. 'You mustn't annoy your father, poor darling; he's in such torment. I'm sure it's the devil. It can't be anything else but evil and the devil trying to dissuade him from the faith.'

Suddenly, they saw each other vividly, but with their shadows grotesquely enlarged and looming over them on the wall. They felt their presences reach beyond them. The Delco had been turned on at the Eccles. They could hear the drone of the generator across the sugarcane fields. It brought a sudden illumination, revealing them and their dark selves, enlarged like on a film screen.

'Run along and have a shower. Get dressed before supper, shoes and socks and a shirt, don't annoy your father. Poor darling.'

'Wrestling with the devil?'

'Quite. Now run along.'

Jonathan turned on the light of his bedroom and looked out of the window where he could hear his father pacing up and down outside, along the gravel avenue of casuarina trees ending in darkness and eternity. Looking out from his own lit room, the darkness was more tangible. He saw his father more clearly in the darkness when he turned the bedroom light off, but he could not see the devil.

He whipped his clothes off for a shower, hurriedly tying a towel around his waist and ran into the kitchen. 'Mummy, I can't see the devil and Dad is walking all alone in the darkness outside.'

'Don't come near this stove in your nakedness. Watch that towel. Now take care and leave the kitchen. Go and wash and bathe yourself before supper. Leave your father alone. You should know better, knowing your catechism the way you do, that you can't see the devil, but that does not mean he doesn't exist.'

She turned to the sink by the window. Then, the scream of her child wrenched her round once more to face him, where he stood next to the stove yelling. His face contorted with absolute terror.

'Mummy, Mummy, Mummy!' Jonathan stood and bawled

and stamped up and down, the pot of boiling rice had tipped over onto his right shoulder and down the side of his body and right leg; the sticky rice clinging to his skin. His face was burnt.

'Darling, my pet,' she brushed off, and picked the pearly grains off his skin, pulling the naked child close to her, his sobs and screams smothered in her lap. 'What has she done? That stupid girl, Sybil, leaving the handle sticking out,' she cried, pushing the blame onto the negligence of the absent servant.

She could see the immediate inflammation and the blisters puckering the child's soft skin.

Then, he fainted. The last words he heard his mother saying were, 'Offer it up, dear.' And then, 'That stupid girl, Sybil.'

Jonathan lay in bed. A white cotton sheet was pulled up over his naked body, tented by a small table, which straddled his legs, so the sheet would not touch the blisters. He was burnt down the right side: thigh, leg and face livid, distended with water blisters. He lay under the white-cotton sheet naked from the waist down.

It seemed that he had to lie like this for an eternity.

The doctor came in the morning. He heard his steps crunching on the gravel. He came to break the water blisters. 'Offer it up now, dear,' his mother said.

Mercy came into the gravel yard lifting her legs. Her steps had another rhythm and she never came up the back stairs. She stayed below, in hell, that black hole of Calcutta. One day, she called from under the window. 'You up there, Master Jonathan? God bless you, child. I bring you some sugar-cake. Sybil go bring it up for you.'

'Yes, Mercy.' He did not know whether she had heard him

from where he lay on his back. 'Thanks, Mercy.'

In the evening there were no more beams of light filtered through the jalousies, and he could not see the tip tops of the flowering palmiste because their green was now part of the darkness. A cool evening breeze came through the window at the same time that his mother came in smelling of eau de Cologne. She patted his forehead with her hanky. He inhaled her.

But still he heard the pacing steps of his father wrestling with the devil, he presumed. He hardly saw him. He would stick his head around the bedroom door before supper. 'You OK, old man?'

Why did he call him old man? He was the old man.

Weeks went by. When would he get better? He would have a scar for life.

Then, one afternoon, the steps on the pitch-pine floor were unfamiliar. They were like someone humping furniture across the drawing room. He had dozed off. The house creaked. The wind whistled outside. Still there was the hump, thump across the drawing room, like someone carrying a bed. His mother was having her siesta. His father was out. He listened as the steps came closer. He thought of the devil that fought with his father. The devil was coming up from his mother's hell.

The steps stopped. He knew someone was at the door. He heard heavy breathing. But lying, looking up at the ceiling where the mosquito net was tied up, he smelt her, the smell of blue soap. He turned his head on the pillow. She was standing, holding on to the door.

'Master Jonathan.'

'Mercy!'

'Yes, is me, boy.'

'You've climbed the stairs, Mercy.'

'So long I not see you, child. I call. You hear me call under the window?'

'Yes, Mercy, I hear you calling me. I call back. You didn't hear me?'

'You voice small, child. And I getting deaf.'

She scratched the inside of her left ear with her index finger. She was bending over the child lying in the bed. On her forehead he saw beads of fresh sweat, beads like his mother's crystal rosary.

'Thanks for the sugar-cake, Mercy.' She smiled and leant over him, smelling of coconut milk.

'Let me see your scar.' She folded back the white cotton sheet. He was shy because she could see his totee. She smiled, recognising his shyness.

'I have boy children too, Master Jonathan, I see my little boys' totee. You lucky the boiling rice didn't burn it off.' She joked and laughed.

Jonathan stared up at the ceiling. The thought of what might have happened, dawning, and the realisation as big as the afternoon sky outside.

'Don't be 'fraid. Don't be shy.' She traced her bony finger round the edges of the largest burn on his thigh. It tickled and itched. With her other hand, she dabbed her neck with a cotton kerchief which smelt of her fresh sweat and bay rum. She patted his brow with it. It made him feel better.

'Take care, child.' Mercy turned, lifting her legs like sticks, and humped them like heavy furniture across the room, disappearing around the door.

'You going to come back up the stairs again, Mercy?'

'No need child, no need.' Her voice echoed and faded as she

humped and thumped across the pitch-pine floor. There was a thunder in the tread of her retreat down the back stairs.

The geography of Jonathan's scars shifted and set. They faded on his arms and legs. The small one on his face disappeared. Only where Mercy had traced her finger, only that jagged map of puckered pink on his thigh, remained.

When he went out to play again, his scar was hidden under his khaki pants. But, when in secret, he looked down at it, noticing what a close shave he had had, he always smelt Mercy's fresh sweat and the bay rum from her hanky. It tickled and itched where Mercy had etched out his scar with her finger.

His father, too, had stopped wrestling with the devil.

And now, the house smelt, not of blue soap and sweat but of coconut milk. The taste on his tongue was sugar-cake.

The Wedding Photograph

'Unheimlich is the name for everything that ought to have remained hidden and secret and has become visible.' *Friedrich Schelling*

'The "uncanny" is that class of the terrifying which leads back to something long known to us, once very familiar. How this is possible, in what circumstances the familiar can become uncanny and frightening, I shall show in what follows.' *Sigmund Freud*

They all looked as if they had seen a ghost.

'The house, where was the house?' she asked, tenacious in her desire for a specific answer, even after all this time, or because of all the time that had passed since that wedding day, and the way things had of disappearing and reappearing in an instant without any warning. 'The house...?' she asked again, 'Where was it?'

The house, with its lowered jalousies, eye-lids closed, the white curtains drawn across the glass window panes, pulled in tightly shut, was its own self, its own veiled face, as if the photographer had not wanted his composition to be distracted by any stray detail which might have emanated from the interior of a bedroom or a dining room; perhaps an unwanted face, or the shadow of a moving figure at his or her tasks within.

'I had a dream, I think, of someone in that house, who...'

Elspeth hesitated, a fearful quaver in her voice.

The house looked both familiar and yet quite strange in the background of the photograph. Something was being both revealed and concealed here by the partial view of this other member of the wedding party: this house.

'I think I still see her. I think…' Elspeth's daydreams, thoughts, were filtered away, her fear interrupting her clarity.

We were looking now at the photograph for the umpteenth time, which was being held on Elspeth's lap by her stiff and shaking fingers, as her body slumped further down into the chair before the fire, and her hold on the past kept slipping away, and then returning with a furious urgency, as she moved from her initial question about the house to a question about the dress.

'There was something about that dress…,' she said, pointing at the little girl at the front of the group photograph who was staring out at us with wide, open eyes, which held a certain sadness, and seemed astonished at what she was seeing in front of her, as she looked across the gravelled yard to what lay beyond.

Elspeth returned to her initial question. 'Where was that house? Who was it…?'

The photograph had been taken in 1927. The wedding group who stood, as if before a firing squad, despite the bride's glimmer of a smile, was composed of the young couple, who became my mother and father; he who was standing stiffly and correctly, prepared for any shot that might be fired at him, and she, his new wife, so demurely on his arm. They stood with the groom's brother on the right of the bride, slightly more at ease with his relaxed shoulders, with his sister beside him, who was one of the bridesmaids. On the left, next to the groom, was another bridesmaid, the bride's best friend. I knew this fact from one of my mother's stories. In front of the groom's brother, standing as it were in wisps of cloud, the burgeoning tulle of the bride's train, masking her shoes and climbing her full white leg-high socks, was the little girl with a bow in her bobbed, black hair, tied with generous ribbons of white satin. Those large and staring eyes did not tell us what she was seeing. She appeared to be in mourning for someone who eluded her.

In the photograph, the walls of the house are thick with vines of honeysuckle, coralita and stephanotis, edged with ferns and tropical palms, providing a dark backdrop to this sepia, in which the colourful flowers are subdued in this noir age of light and shadow, and in which the bouquets, held in the arms of the bride and bridesmaids, are also the diminished and muted but generous blooms of orchids, lilies and asparagus ferns; so yellowed by the photography of the day and the passage of time that it is left to us now to imagine the heat and the vibrancy of that world's colours. The white and creamy textures of the bridesmaids' dresses and hats, the bride's veil, decorated with embroidery and lace, are a contrast to the raffia-patterned carpet, which lies on the bare ground for the arrangement of the bride's train. The foreground is the gravelled yard with the shadows of trees, not in the photograph, but just beyond the frame, growing in the pasture of the cocoa estate beyond: those shadows had accumulated there on this sunny afternoon of the wedding day. The blemishes in the photograph, now, are the blemishes of age.

'I don't think she wore that dress to the wedding,' Elspeth said shakily, pointing at the little girl, her unsteady finger unable to keep its aim, slipping across the photograph, the way a needle on an old record-player had of suddenly jumping out of its groove and skating across the vinyl, sounding a discordant note, a screech, and then leaving an irreparable scratch.

'What do you mean?' I asked. 'Do you mean that this photograph was taken before the wedding, or after the wedding, for that matter, and she wore this dress solely for the photograph, but did not go to the wedding in it? Why would she do that? Who made her do that? Who would have dressed her in this way for one event and then dressed her differently for another?'

Elspeth followed my rapid, circuitous questions with difficulty, her eyes seeming to search for my meaning and her own at the same time, for both our questions and any possible answers there might still be in the layers of memory, whose seams were still left to be mined.

'Something like that...,' she answered. Then, with more certainty, and vigour in her voice, she asked: 'How can we shed any light on this darkness now?' She was shaking at that moment with fear, or her Parkinson's erupting momentarily. There was still an hour to go before her five o'clock pill.

'You were asking about the house. Do you still not recognise where it was? Was it not at El Salvador?'

'Was it? I would very much like to find out. And ...'

'Yes...?

I wondered why it was so important for her to fix on this detail of the house; the little girl's dress seemed a much more easily understood interest. The house must have been so familiar once, what went on inside and what lay beyond the pastures.

It was now puzzling her, eluding her, haunting her memory. Did she not remember where she had grown up? I looked at it again, so shut up, it gave away very little about itself. What were its secrets, its ghosts?

Of course, any detail might be important to fix on, if everything was disappearing and then reappearing without control; the vagaries of a deteriorating mind. Usually, with Elspeth, memories from this long ago were as vivid as yesterday, while the happenings of yesterday had completely disappeared.

But it seemed as if this ghost of the past would not appear to her or stay long enough to explain itself. It was not even as vivid as it was in the sepia world which had by now slipped to the floor, and which I had to retrieve, so that we could carry on with our examination of the past through the photographs from the old family album.

'There you are,' I said, lifting the photograph from the floor and replacing it on Elspeth's lap for her continued inspection. 'Do you remember the day at all, the wedding ceremony, the reception?'

'No, not at all. Not now. It's all gone. They're all gone now,' she answered decisively. More and more she spoke with her eyes closed, too tired to keep them open and focussed. It occurred to me that we were dealing with a kind of blindness at this moment.

'But the dress, you remember that, don't you?'

'Yes, yes. But, the house…?' She repeated her affirmative to convince herself, and then returned to her persistent question about the house, her rheumy eyes fluttering open and then closing again, but giving away very little information. She was as locked up as the house itself.

How reliable were any of these memories? What in fact

could a memory be of, at this point in time, given Elspeth's state of mind?

I held one edge of the photograph to prevent it from falling to the floor again with Elspeth's persistent shaking; and we both stared at the little girl once more.

'How old were you then?'

'I can't remember.'

I was beginning to see that this was her easy answer, but that with time, there was the possibility of the retrieval of fragments, which needed to be composed into a coherent narrative. Then, maybe, the ghosts of the house might reappear: the ghost story might get told.

We continued to stare at the little girl. I looked more carefully at the dress. The white sleeveless shift hung daintily from her small, narrow shoulders, a corsage of tightly gathered flowers, little buds, roses maybe, was pinned on the strap of her left shoulder; the dress heavily embroidered and trimmed with lace cut into diamond patterns, nineteen-twenties style. I could hear a jazzy music in the fold and fall of the skirt, an echo of the dance and the swirl of the dancers. She wore a chain with a pendant.

The little girl was my elderly cousin. She was now nearly a century old. It was hard to imagine such a long time. The havoc, which that passage of time had played with her health, was plain to see. I wondered what else time had affected.

She had once been that pretty little girl with her large black eyes staring out at whatever lay beyond. I did wonder about the photographer. He clearly hadn't said, 'Cheese.' If he had, there hadn't been a response. I imagined him ducking in and out from under the canopy of his standing camera, rickety on its tripod on the gravelled surface of the yard. Was he one of those photographers from the studios on Coffee Street in San

Fernando, Wong's, where we had all gone on various anniversaries to be photographed? Maybe it was that tiny explosion, that puff, as the shot was taken, that had them all looking so surprised, as if they'd seen a ghost.

'You must've been four or five at the time,' I suggested.

'I can't remember. Yes, I must've been.'

'The year is 1927. You were born in 1923, yes?'

'Really? I can't remember.'

'You look a little sad.'

'I must've been.'

'Why was that?'

I knew some of her story, but I thought it might help her mind to tell it again.

'My mother…,' she said. 'She went away to England and left me behind.' She then seemed to digress, to choose another path, or be chosen by another random memory: 'Well, there was a school. And we got beaten on the hand. You had to put out your hand to be beaten with a ruler.'

'Gosh, you remember that now?' I was still to understand the logic within which her mind now worked, or, as it could seem at times, possessed, something other than herself designing the trajectory of her thoughts.

'Yes, very well, very clearly.'

'What else do you remember?'

'I remember an uncle. I called him "Boo".'

'Boo?'

'Yes, whenever he came to the house he would enter the room, and if I was there, he would poke his head around the door exclaiming, "Boo!"' Elspeth laughed with her memory. 'I was excited, and sometimes afraid. I would hide behind the couch. So, I called him Uncle Boo. And then I think everyone in the family called him Boo from that time onwards. Uncle

Boo.'

'Such a long time ago.'

'They come and go...'

Many of her sentences remained unfinished.

'Yes.'

'Like ghosts...'

'That is what we say. An odd idea.'

My visit had come to an end. Elspeth's carer, returning from her break, administered the five o'clock pill. In time, her shaking would subside, and possibly those fragmented memories might become whole again for a short period.

I left to catch my train.

Our conversation was resumed a fortnight later. I had gained the reputation over the weeks of being someone she particularly looked forward to talking with because I could take her back to the past of her childhood in Trinidad. This was so far back that it allowed her a clarity that eluded her carers, who, as kind as they were, had little that could engage those triggers of her memory, which still worked. She must have been terribly confused about the rest of her life, because I would hardly call it clarity, which we had so far managed during my visits.

She was often in a frustrated state when I arrived. She reminded me of a small child who does not get her questions answered. There were, briefly, the glimpses of the middle-aged woman I used to know who had been in full command of her life.

'Have I got any relatives?'

Elspeth greeted me with this astonishing question after I had brought in tea and biscuits on a tray and settled myself in the buttoned chair next to her, arranging my outstretched legs, so that they did not hamper the movement of her walking frame.

'Of course, you have relatives. I'm a relative. Here are your grandsons.' I handed her a photograph from off the mantlepiece.

'Really!'

'Yes, and your daughter.'

'Yes, of course.'

She knew her daughter, the mainstay of her life who lived around the corner and visited every day.

Elspeth sipped tea and nibbled on one of the chocolate biscuits.

'Who do they think I am?' she whispered, leaning over to me conspiratorially. Then the same question was reframed as, 'Who am I?'

'Who do you mean, "they" and what do you mean, "Who am I?"' I wasn't expecting us to launch into existential metaphysics this afternoon. We were now on another track. Or, were we? Quite soon I could see that these seemingly philosophical questions were directly related to the conversation that we had been having during my previous visit on the whereabouts of the house in the wedding photograph.

'I mean. Who am I? Where did I come from? There were other relatives, other people in my life. This is recent,' she said, looking about her small London flat with the mementos and photographs of her children and grandchildren, and of her late husband.

I noticed that there were no memories of Trinidad. The walls were hung with views of Suffolk and Somerset.

Sometimes she would become a bit sleepy after I had first arrived, but not this afternoon. She was fully awake and in hot pursuit of her subject, and ordering me to fetch her another cup of tea, though I could detect a rising fear in her voice.

What had frightened her? What had brought this on?

Her carer was back and I had to leave to catch a train. I mentioned the obsession to Marjorie as I left. She told me that Elspeth had been obsessed the past week with these questions of her other relatives, other people who had been important in her life. Marjorie did not know how to respond, how to try and calm her mind. 'It's as if she's being persecuted. Or, as if she's possessed.'

'Hardly,' I said. 'Possibly the effect of those pills, those drugs.'

'You know she keeps asking about the dark woman and the baby in a basket.'

'Which dark woman and which baby in a basket?'

'I don't know. I thought you might.'

I left, puzzling over the dark woman and the baby in the basket.

Once, quite sometime back, when Elspeth was a well woman, in full command of her mind, she gave me an old map of Trinidad and pointed out the spot, marked with an x next to the name, El Salvador, the family's cocoa estate in the south of the island. I was making one of my annual visits back home and Elspeth wanted me to find the old estate and the same house, which was in the wedding photograph, and to report to her in what condition I found the place, particularly the house. I wondered then if some of the ghosts, that were appearing and disappearing both day and night in the small flat in London, might have first of all arisen there, in that house. Were they trapped there in her imagination or memory? Was that from where the dark woman and the baby in the basket entered the story? They must have been some of the familiar memories of the house and her life there as a child.

Then the figures of the women and the little girl in the wedding photograph in their lace and tulle, the men in their fitted dark suits, appeared and disappeared and reappeared again for me, as they did in Elspeth's mind, to haunt the reflections I was continuing to have as I travelled home and back again to London.

I thought of the shadows of the large samaans I found there, at El Salvador, and of the similar shadows, which had accumulated on the gravelled yard in the wedding photograph. They were shading large patches of the pastures of the old estate, tucked away off the Manahambre Road, which wound its way among the sugarcane fields of Indian Walk on its way to Bande l'Est where we used to go on holidays to Mayaro, to a house set among the dunes and coconut palms.

Did the photograph, and others like it, which depicted such an elegant and graceful life, have hidden in it for Elspeth, beneath its surface, as if a palimpsest, another story, the one perhaps which lay behind the shuttered windows of the house in the wedding photograph, the walls of which were overgrown with honeysuckle, coralita and stephanotis; those same windows firmly shut and curtained off?

The familiar had become strange. The familiar was haunting Elspeth.

On my next visit, I found her already up from her rest and sitting waiting for me in the living room of her small, but smartly appointed flat. The afternoon sun was pouring in through the French windows. Marjorie had already laid a tray for tea and there was this afternoon a slice of cake, Victoria sponge, as well as the usual chocolate biscuits.

I noticed that there was an envelope on her tray. She kept stretching out to touch it. I expected there to be some new revelation. 'I have found something I must show you,' she said urgently.

I did not want in any way to inhibit her train of thought, interrupt what with Elspeth now seemed a kind of free-association journey as she spoke whatever came into her mind, struggling to find meaning and give meaning to what could sound like oracular utterances at times.

Elspeth, blinking, caught in the light of an English summer's afternoon after cups of tea in the bright sunshine streaming through from the small balcony, seemed instead, now, to be silenced by her discovery. I did not want to press her. I restrained my curiosity.

I left that afternoon wondering about the discovery, which was still a secret. She had not shown me what was in the envelope. What other ghosts were there from El Salvador, which had come to roam around her London flat, returning to terrify her in her weaker moments at night, and in that four o'clock striking of the village church chime, and waking her at dawn.

I wondered what I would find on my next visit.

I had a copy of the same original wedding photograph in my own family archive. I sat at home the next day examining the detail. The factual certainties, which photographs represent, can sometimes mask what else we might know of a time, so that the photograph seems a fiction. What was the truth, which lay beneath the surface of that photograph?

I imagined the scene in the shuttered house; the black

seamstress working round the clock to get ready for the wedding, the little flower-girl's dress being the last to be done. Was it the trial of the trying on? Had there been a tantrum, having to stand still while being pinned, and the anticipation of the whole ceremony ahead, the getting to the church, the walk up the aisle, the carrying of the train, the arranging of the train? Had there been hot tears that afternoon? Was it all too much for the little girl without her mother's protection, standing still and sitting still in the hushed church for so long?

I can well imagine, drawing from my own experience of childhood at a later date, the panic that that could cause; the fainting fits that might be provoked in hot, still churches, in the crush of an over-scented congregation. She may have broken down in tears, had had the feeling of carrying all the responsibility for her favourite aunt's wedding day.

Whether ghosts existed or not could be debated. I'm sure Elspeth would agree with me that that they were not likely, just as the supernatural and after-life was probably not likely either. These resurrected memories had more in them, it seemed, to terrify than any of the ghost stories she had been told as a small child living in her grandparents' house with her mother far away in England at the time.

Elspeth's story had returned to haunt me over the weeks I did not see her, while I once more travelled back to Trinidad. It was when I was there that my imagination and my memory drew on the fertility which geography can provide. My mother had told me the story of her childhood. I could not imagine nor remember what it might be that was particular for Elspeth concerning the house at El Salvador.

While standing in the middle of the estate yard at El Salvador with what remained of the cocoa houses and the remnants of the great estate house and the overseer's house, I tried to recall what it might have seemed like to the little girl in 1927 at the front of the wedding photograph staring out, bewildered.

The sequel to this part of Elspeth's story is that she did not remember her mother's return to Trinidad to eventually collect her daughter and take her to England. It was my belief that Elspeth's recent panic and fear had originated in this terrible estrangement, abandonment as a small child, who would have experienced her mother's absence from Trinidad as a kind of death.

When I returned to England and went to visit Elspeth, having had the news that she had nearly died twice from pneumonia in my absence, I was taken with complete surprise by what greeted me in Elspeth's current preoccupations, obsessions and new ghosts. She had achieved something like clarity.

As was usual, it was after tea and biscuits when Elspeth's lucidity was at its best. Her question seemed to have come from some long reflection while I had been away. But now that I think of it, her question must have been formed during my descriptions of El Salvador, which she was anxious to hear about. She remembered the map and she remembered the estate and particularly the house.

She jumped ahead of me with her question. Or, was it that she was going back to something that horrified her more than any of the other ghosts, which we had discussed over the months?

She picked up the envelope, which had not been opened on our previous meetings. 'Here are our answers.' She extracted three photographs and handed them to me. I noticed that the envelope was labelled, 'Old Nurse, Most Important.' The photographs, small black and white snaps, showed a black woman in white apron and cap, ready for duty, and the little girl, Elspeth, at her side.

'She knew the house. She knew everything that went on in the house,' Elspeth insisted. 'She also knew what went on beyond the pasture in the barrack yards.'

Elspeth returned now, as if she were actually there, knowing the door that did not open easily, the cupboard that creaked, the bolt that had to be hammered for it to open to get into the attic. 'I can hear again the drip drip of the tap near the bed of ferns and anthurium lilies.' She spoke as if she could feel the very pulse of the house, a throbbing pulse, repeating its mantra: *Home Home.*

'Old Nurse repeated their names, the names which she told me used to be written on lists in the ledgers of the estate, the lists of all the people who had worked on the estate and who were buried beyond the pasture without any names. 'Nowhere,' she used to say, 'are their names written down, but in my memory.'

How had Elspeth achieved this measure of clarity? My own answer was the envelope of photographs, labelled, 'Old Nurse, Most Important.'

'She enumerated from memory, actual names...' Elspeth continued with her new story.

'Of those who had been enslaved?'

'Yes, some, and those who came after.'

Elspeth opened her eyes wide as if to try her utmost to see, and to tell me the encompassing truth that had determined the fortunes of her ancestors. It was something which that little bewildered child at the front of the wedding photograph seemed to be seeing without fully understanding her place in that history. Elspeth was drawn now to places she had been taken as a child where generations lay side by side: mothers, fathers and children without names.

'There were no names like there would be names on graves, or in a family Bible. The names had been in registers in dated ledgers, 1820-1838, long ago, lost. I repeated after Old Nurse, those names, tasks, punishments, and the number of lashes, which were noted in the earliest of the ledgers,' she told me.

I had not heard Elspeth be so lucid for months.

She told me then of how Old Nurse would take her, at night, into the moonlit yard, across the muddy ditch, into the barrack yards where the drumming came from at night. There she saw the women in white with turbans of white cotton, in their dance, opening and closing like large flowers, or, as she elaborated, like the wings of enormous butterflies, taking flight. She watched their naked feet on the bare ground stepping through their dance to the drums. These memories crowded her London flat and came to live with her. These were the people she had not been able to remember. Their absence had frightened her. Old Nurse was that relative she was trying to recall, who had returned now to comfort her in the absence of her mother's protection.

But now, in this state of appearing and disappearing memories, the ghosts of all those in the enumerated lists written in the estate registers, seemed to congregate all around her, repeating their names as if in some litany of prayer.

'My God!' Elspeth exclaimed. 'Extraordinary. They were real people. I saw them in their dances entering the circle of the yard with elegance and departing with grace, only to enter again, back and forth.'

'Yes, you must've, when you were that little girl in the wedding photograph.'

'Yes, I must've. I can't remember.'

'But you have, with your questions, just now, these months, and now with these photographs of Old Nurse.'

'Yes, I must've...Yes, she comes to comfort me at night, carrying me, a baby in a basket.'

Elspeth smiled, seemingly satisfied that she had at last remembered something that had been bothering her for a long time. This knowledge settled her, took her fear away.

'Another cup of tea?'

We sat back, sipping tea and eating chocolate biscuits. The wedding photograph was on the side-table between us, the little girl staring out beyond the pastures of the estate house at El Salvador, looking at what was familiar, and finding in that memory of the estates and their workers a haunting. They had become the saving presences of people she once knew, relatives, real people, whom Old Nurse made her understand and remember. If she had stayed in Trinidad and not left for England, she would not have lost them. They no longer frightened her now, but instead, comforted her, coming to the edge of her bed at night in her London flat to perform their dance to the gentle drums, which used to come across the pasture in the moonlight when she was a little girl.

Acknowledgements

Many of these stories have appeared in slightly different versions in journals and anthologies, or have been read on the BBC. *Faith's Pilgrimage* (1997); *Ash on Guavas* (1997); *The Archbishop's Egg* (1997); *A Little Something* (then entitled, *From the Cane*, 2006) were read on BBC Radio 4, while *A 1930s Tale: Coco's Last Christmas* was read on BBC Radio 3 (1994), a version of which was part of my novel *Night Calypso* (Allison & Busby, 2004). I wish to acknowledge the producers Pamela Fraser-Solomon and Julian May and the editor David Shelley. *Leaving by Plane Swimming back Underwater* appeared in a very different version in *God* (Serpent's Tail, 1992). I acknowledge the editors Stephen Hayward and Sarah Lafanu. Stories published in journals include: *Mercy* (Trinidad & Tobago Review, 1995); *The Archbishop's Egg* (Trinidad & Tobago Review, 1996); *Mercy* was also published in The Routledge Reader (1996). I would like to acknowledge the editors, Keith Jardim, Alison Donnell and Sarah Lawson Welsh. *Ash on Guavas* was published in Bomb Magazine NY (2002-2003); *A Little Something* (as *From the Cane*), in *Moving Worlds* (2011); *Prophet* in *Trinidad Noir* (Akashic Books NY, 2008); *The Penalty of Death* (Wasafiri, 2013); *Tales Told Under the San Fernando Hill* in *The Cross-Dressed Caribbean* (University of Virginia Press, 2014). I acknowledge the editors: Betsy Sussler, Shirley Chew, Lucy Evans, Lisa Allen-Agostini, Jeanne Mason, Stephanie Decouvelaere, Malachi McIntosh, Maria Cristina Fumagali, Benedicte Ledent and Roberto del Valle Alcala. I acknowledge quotes from WH Auden's *Musée des Beaux Arts* (Copyright © 1940 by W.H. Auden, renewed. Reprinted by permission of Curtis Brown, Ltd), Martin Carter's *This is the Dark Time, My Love* and Tom Lowenstein's *Filibustering in Samsara*, Phyllis Shand Allfrey's *Love for an Island*, David Rudder's *Laventille*, Bob Dylan's *We Shall Overcome* and *Blowing in the Wind*; also for the use of extracts from the hymns *Rock of Ages* and *Sweet Sacrament Divine*. My thanks to Sue Wincent Dodd for advice on the Swedish language.

I am grateful for the support of Romesh Gunesekera and Elizabeth Walcott-Hackshaw. I would like to thank my agent Andrew Hewson at Johnson & Alcock for his continuing encouragement and sound judgement. I am thrilled that the stories have found a home at Papillote Press and my special thanks goes to its editor, Polly Pattullo, for her generosity of spirit and sensitive attention. Above all, my thanks to Jenny Green, my collaborator in so many ways.

About the author

Lawrence Scott is a prize-winning novelist and short-story writer from Trinidad & Tobago. He was awarded a Lifetime Literary award in 2012 by the National Library of Trinidad & Tobago for his significant contribution to the literature of Trinidad & Tobago. His most recent novel *Light Falling on Bamboo* (2012) received an honourable mention from Casa de las Americas prize, Cuba, 2014; longlisted for the International Impac Dublin literary award, 2014; a special mention from the Grand Prix Littéraire de l'Association des Ecrivains de la Caraïbe from the Congrès des Ecrivains de la Caraïbe, Guadeloupe, 2013; shortlisted for the OCM BOCAS prize fiction category and longlisted for the overall OCM BOCAS prize, 2013. His second novel *Aelred's Sin* (1998) was awarded a Commonwealth Writers' prize, Best Book in Canada and the Caribbean, and was longlisted for the International Impac Dublin Literary award, 1999. His first novel *Witchbroom* (1992) was shortlisted for a Commonwealth Writers' prize, 1993, Best First Book, and was read as a BBC Book At Bedtime, 1994. His short-story collection *Ballad for the New World* (1994) included the Tom-Gallon Trust prize-winning short story, *The House of Funerals*. His novel *Night Calypso* (2004) was also shortlisted for a Commonwealth Writers' Prize, Best Book award, and longlisted for the International IMPAC Dublin Literary award, 2005, and translated into French as *Calypso de Nuit* (2005). It was a One Book One Community choice in 2006 by the National Library of Trinidad & Tobago. He is the editor of

Golconda: Our Voices Our Lives, an anthology of oral histories and other stories and poems from the sugar-belt in Trinidad (UTT Press, 2009). Over the years, he has combined teaching with writing. He lives in London and Port of Spain and can be found at www.lawrencescott.co.uk.